"WILLOW!"

Goosebumps crawled onto Will[illegible]
heard the cold, raspy voi[illegible] of
the baby's room.

"An apology isn't acc[illegible]ble," Cordelia was saying through the phone. "Just because I hang out with Buffy and you guys staking the occasional vampire and whatever would-be monster or ancient curse that happens to come along doesn't mean we're anywhere near the same social level. You—"

Willow turned back to the crib. The flashlight beam played over Baby Tad.

He was sitting up, his little round head too big for his body. He looked like an unfinished sculpture, kind of soft and doughy around the edges, the way all babies did. He wore a Mickey Mouse sleeper. But his eyes glowed hot green like molten jade. A look of pure evil filled them.

"Willow," Tad said again, milky drool trickling down the side of his chin. "We need to talk."

Buffy the Vampire Slayer™

Buffy the Vampire Slayer (movie tie-in)
The Harvest
Halloween Rain
Coyote Moon
Night of the Living Rerun
The Angel Chronicles, Vol. 1
Blooded
The Angel Chronicles, Vol. 2
The Xander Years, Vol. 1
Visitors
Unnatural Selection

Available from ARCHWAY Paperbacks

Buffy the Vampire Slayer adult books

Child of the Hunt
Return to Chaos
The Gatekeeper Trilogy
    Book 1: Out of the Madhouse
    Book 2: Ghost Roads
    Book 3: Sons of Entropy

The Watcher's Guide: The Official Companion to the Hit Show
The Postcards
The Essential Angel

Available from POCKET BOOKS

BUFFY
THE VAMPIRE
SLAYER™

UNNATURAL SELECTION

Mel Odom
An original novel based on the hit TV series
created by Joss Whedon

AN ARCHWAY PAPERBACK
Published by POCKET BOOKS
New York London Toronto Sydney Tokyo Singapore

AN ARCHWAY PAPERBACK *Original*

An Archway Paperback published by
POCKET BOOKS, a division of Simon & Schuster Inc.
1230 Avenue of the Americas, New York, NY 10020

ISBN: 0-671-02630-5

First Archway Paperback printing June 1999

10 9 8 7 6 5 4 3 2

Printed and bound in Great Britain by
Omnia Books Ltd, Glasgow
IL 15+

For Sherry
> My friend and my love,
> Who found
> Dreams in my heart,
> Then gave them wing
> And all of the sky.

And for Lisa Clancy and Liz Shiflett
> Friends and editors,
> Who believe in fun
> That comes from work well done.
> Thanks for keeping me
> On the page
> And between the lines.
> And for all the Crayons!

ACKNOWLEDGMENTS

To Joss Whedon and the cast and crew of *Buffy the Vampire Slayer,* for a show about high school students who are going to have some of the neatest stories to tell their children. I'm waiting for the twentieth anniversary show when their offspring are talking to each other.

Student: So, Xander, what'd your dad say when you told him you tanked the history test?

Xander, Jr.: Man, he gave me that same old story. "When I was your age, I had to stake vampires all night, wrap up the mummy girl, beat down zombies, *and* pass a history test. Uphill both ways and through the snow. What's your excuse?"

UNNATURAL SELECTION

CHAPTER 1

A short, muffled bump echoed inside the Campbells' big Victorian-style house and drew Willow Rosenberg's attention immediately from the medieval text in her lap. She looked around the living room. *Other people's houses and the noises that go with them . . . on the next* Lifestyles of the Weird and Eerie.

She felt bad immediately because the Campbells were good people. They couldn't help it if their house made strange noises and she was getting creeped out while baby-sitting. And they couldn't help it if her life had taken a turn for the weird side of life that made every shadow suspicious.

She'd automatically reached for the bookbag at her feet rather than the cordless phone on the couch beside her. Experience had taught her the wooden stake in the bookbag might keep her alive against things that went bump in the night longer than dialing 911 would.

In Sunnydale, situated over the Hellmouth that allowed nearly any nightmarish *thing* to take shape, the police often couldn't help—or didn't.

The large picture window across the room overlooked the Campbells' flower gardens and greenhouse. Usually, like now, the backyard resembled a jungle. Luminescent pale yellow and white moonflowers as big as her hand reflected the brightness of the waning moon.

Did something move out there? Willow peered through the glass, and through her own reflection painted on the glass by the glow of the lamp on the end table next to the couch. *And if it did, would I see it?*

And would it see me?

The flowers and the trees rippled in the gentle wind. All the movement seemed natural.

Willow let out a short sigh of relief. She let go the wooden stake. *Just get a grip. You're tired and it's been a long time since you've been in this house. You're just creeping yourself out because you've got a friend with a really strange job.*

The living room was large, filled with overstuffed furniture from the 1940s Willow remembered from past times when she'd baby-sat for the Campbells. Even the entertainment center and console television were rendered in the baroque style of the time. A Discovery Channel presentation on the Amazon jungle she'd seen before was on the television, but she kept it on for company.

To be on the safe side, she went upstairs to check on the baby. The happy clown face night-light revealed him in a soft glow. Tad Campbell was eight months old, with curly blond hair and big green eyes. When he was awake. He was still sleeping now, one tiny fist pressed to his mouth.

Now that's a Kodak moment.

Willow went back downstairs and opened her book again. The page she was on showed drawings of medieval torture devices and intense narrative descriptions of their use. *Not exactly light bedtime reading,* she thought lifting her diet soda from the coaster on the end table and taking a sip. She almost choked when she heard the short, muffled *bump* repeated. This time she was certain it came from upstairs, not outside.

Don't wig yet, she told herself. *That could have been a cat or a branch, or something else.*

Her mind seemed to really lock on the *something else* possibility. The more she thought about it, the bigger the *something* got. *Evil things do tend to grow . . . when they have a supply of victims.* She put the book down and stood, listening intently.

She flicked the toggle on the intercom system, bringing up the baby's room. It was set to automatically come on whenever the baby made noise. So far, Tad had slept all night. She heard nothing.

Flicking the toggle off and knowing she was too weirded to calmly sit by without hearing the sound of someone else's voice, she went upstairs and checked on the baby again. Still sleeping.

Back downstairs, she grabbed the cordless phone

and dialed Buffy's number. *C'mon, c'mon, be there. Every little vampire's back in its grave for the evening, right?* She paced the living room as she waited.

"Hello?"

"Oh, hello," Willow gasped, recognizing the voice. "Mrs. Summers, it's Willow. I was calling for Buffy."

"I'm sorry. Buffy's not here at the moment."

No! She has to be. Okay, deep breath. Do the calm thing. "When do you expect her back?"

"She didn't say."

The way Buffy's mom said that let Willow know Buffy was out doing Slayer things, things Mrs. Summers was aware of but sometimes couldn't acknowledge outright. *Like maybe Buffy was going to run into the one vampire that was too fast for the Slayer and not come home at all. At least, not without really bad skin, big teeth, and a whole new drink of choice.* Willow felt guilty about not going with Buffy that night, but she knew Buffy still did a lot of solo runs against the vamps.

"Willow, are you okay?"

"I'm fine. Really." The last thing Willow wanted was for Buffy's mom to flip out and tell Buffy that something might be wrong with her. It wouldn't be good for Buffy to show up at the Campbells' house after staking the latest fangers only to find out Willow was imagining things. "I was just . . . calling to . . . uh, ask her when she wanted to . . . get together for the tutoring she asked about." That was believable. Buffy sometimes struggled with her grades because of her *extracurricular* activities.

"I'll tell her you called."

"No. That's okay. Thanks Mrs. Summers, but I'll just talk to her tomorrow." *Like tomorrow's not going to be too late.* Willow said good-bye and broke the connection. She still felt creeped out and didn't want to sit down.

My spider senses are tingling, Xander would say.

She glanced at the clock on the VCR. It was 9:28 P.M. The Campbells wouldn't be home for another hour and a half. Every bad teen slasher/baby-sitter movie Xander had ever talked her into seeing flashed through her head.

She decided to call Oz. He always made her feel calm. He was just that kind of a guy, in spite of being a part-time werewolf. He was rehearsing with his band tonight, but she knew he'd talk to her.

The bump sounded again while the phone rang.

Buffy Summers moved surefootedly through the darkness constantly scanning the forest around her. Her Slayer senses were more acute than a normal person's, but not paying attention was not paying attention. In her work, not paying attention could get her killed. She was quiet as a whisper gliding through a mausoleum.

Her companion wasn't nearly so silent. Rupert Giles was a librarian and her Watcher. Though his training was specialized so he could in turn train her, he hadn't been born with the special physical attributes of the Slayer. He stepped on yet another branch that cracked loud enough to wake the dead.

Or the undead in this case, Buffy thought, glancing

back at him long enough to make sure it was a misstep and not an attack.

"Sorry," he whispered. "Walking around in this darkness is beastly."

"Yeah, well you're going to see how beastly it can get if you don't tread a little lighter there, Pathfinder."

"Ah." Giles was complimented despite the present mission. "I see you've been doing American literature studies. But I didn't know they were covering James Fenimore Cooper's tales of Natty Bumppo."

"Extra credit, Giles," Buffy replied, sighing. *I've learned to live for extra credit.* "I kind of tanked the last Lit test." She was dressed for the night, wearing black leggings, boots, and a stylish crocheted shirt over a black crop top. Her backpack held the gear she'd packed for the patrol.

"I thought you studied for that test."

"I did," Buffy said, "but that was also during the week those rockabilly vampires from Tennessee came to Sunnydale tracking down Elvis memorabilia." *Definitely not a restful week.*

"Right." In the shadow of a nearby tree, only Giles's blue pinstriped shirt and gold-rimmed glasses were visible.

"They killed three people before I found them." Buffy ducked under the lowest branches of the oak tree, following the game trail she'd discovered. "It's kind of hard balancing the Slaying thing and getting study time."

"I didn't mean to sound like I was taking you to task for your grades."

Giles is tired too, Buffy realized. "Look, it's no sweat. The extra work I'm doing is pulling my grade back up from that test." *Slowly.*

"Let me know if I can help. James Fenimore Cooper told rather a rousing tale."

Rousing? Buffy thought with a smile, but she continued along the game trail. Out from under the trees in the moonlight, the trail was almost visible to the normal naked eye. "Thanks, Giles, but for now it's just me and Cliff."

Giles stumbled over a loose branch. "Cliff?"

"Buy a clue, Giles," Buffy said. "Cliff as in Cliff Notes. I read the book; I read the study guide; I do the paper. Extra credit."

"I see. You've been busy lately."

"I'm always busy, Giles. It just seems more so lately." *He doesn't notice because he's been doing the Watcher gig a lot longer than I've been a Slayer.* Movement attracted her attention to her left, but she didn't break her stride. The night was filled with hunters. She was merely one of them. *Only the best survive, though.*

"Have you had any luck finding out why the vampires seem to be so interested in this park?" Giles asked. He'd come along to offer another perspective on the recurring problem.

"No, and I haven't exactly figured out how to handle the Cordy/Willow situation about the Spring Blow-Out coming up this weekend either." *Staking vampires is easy compared to that, and maybe less dangerous.*

Movement flashed again to the left. *Low to the ground and definitely bigger than a breadbox.* Buffy tracked it but kept moving. Sometimes in order to hunt best, a hunter had to pretend to be hunted. *Giles taught me that. Or was it Angel?*

"I wasn't aware there was a situation other than the presence of the vampires."

"Hello? How do you miss these things? Cordy's organizing the Blow-Out and Willow's against the sale of the park to the land developers. Big conflict of interest. Huge, even. Haven't you noticed the tension?"

"No," Giles said honestly.

"Both of them want my help, but I don't know what I'm supposed to do."

"What do you want to do?"

"I'd like to go to the Spring Blow-Out," Buffy said. "But if Willow gets her way we probably won't have it. Either way spending my school break staking vampires here in Weatherly Park didn't show up anywhere on my wish list."

"No. I suppose it didn't."

Most of Buffy's attention was on the movement to the left. *There's more than one of them moving in the trees. This is about to get really interesting.* Despite the fear that thrilled around inside her, she still felt a little excited. She slid her hand into her backpack and gripped the crossbow stock. *Come on, boys . . .*

Buffy moved ahead again, more slowly. She felt their eyes on her now. Even without her beefed-up Slayer senses and skills she'd have felt them. They stared with the same intensity of sixth-grade boys who'd just noticed girls were different. Crimson eyes glinted in the darkness as they closed in. She grabbed the front of Giles's jacket in one hand and jerked him to one side just as the lead vampire leaped.

She twisted and rolled, barely avoiding the rush from the second one. Its fetid breath pushed against her cheek and its talons raked her hair. Coming to her feet, she brought the crossbow to her shoulder and fired.

The bolt crossed the twelve-foot distance and split the vampire's dead heart. The creature threw its head back and screamed defiantly. But it was wasted effort. The wooden shaft piercing its heart reduced it to an explosion of ashes in seconds.

Buffy didn't have time to celebrate her victory, though. The other vampires rushed at them from the trees. She grabbed Giles by the arm and shoved him ahead of her.

"Run!" she ordered.

The vampire pack howled at their heels.

"Hi. May I speak to Oz, please?" Willow gripped the phone tightly. She listened intently for the bump to repeat.

At the other end of the connection she heard a rumble of voices, someone picking deliberate notes on a guitar, the rat-a-tat-tat of snare drums, and music playing in the background. The band always rehearsed casually.

Willow checked the intercom to the baby's room again. She heard nothing. *At least Tad's sleeping through this.*

"Hey," Oz said into the phone.

"How's practice going?" Willow asked. *Man, just one word, one syllable from Oz and I'm already getting a whole new perspective on things.* Now that she actually had Oz on the phone she felt better. She also felt calling him about a couple of bumps was maybe a little flaky.

"Good," Oz said minimalist as always. "So what's up?"

He always knows when to listen. Willow paced the living room. *Why doesn't the bump sound now? So I can say, See, that's what's freaking me out.* "I guess I'm a little nervous."

"About baby-sitting? You told me you'd baby-sat for the Campbells before."

"Sure. A couple years ago when Bobby was small." The older Campbell boy was at a sleepover tonight.

"Is Tad that much different?"

Willow smiled. Oz always had a good memory. She knew most guys let whatever a girl told them slip right through their heads. Even though Xander usually remembered everything, he didn't always listen as attentively as Oz did. "No. In fact I've only changed him once. He's been asleep all evening."

"Did you get the chance to talk to Mr. Campbell?"

"No." Actually, getting asked to watch Tad Campbell when the regular baby-sitter called in sick had gotten Willow's spirits up. She'd really wanted the chance to lobby Mr. Campbell against the proposed zoning changes that would allow Gallivan Industries to tear down Weatherly Park. *It's something Cordy would do if she had the opportunity.* "He was in a big hurry tonight."

"Don't give up on it," Oz encouraged.

"I won't. Weatherly Park has a lot of memories for me and other kids. I don't want to see the park torn down. Even to make room for a new amusement park. Those you can get anywhere, but Weatherly Park is one of a kind."

Someone called Oz's name at the other end of the connection. "Be there in a minute," Oz said.

"Are you guys going somewhere?" Willow asked, hoping Oz would say no.

"We thought we'd grab a pizza then get back and work another couple hours," Oz said. "Unless you need something?"

"No." The bump hadn't been repeated. Willow kept pacing. *I'm not going to ask unless I know for sure something weird is going on.* She glanced at the intercom, realizing something was bothering her but frustrated because she didn't know what it was. "I guess . . . I guess I just wanted to hear your voice." *And that's true too.*

"It's always good to hear yours," Oz told her.

Willow smiled, and suddenly the fear that had been knocking around inside her seemed to be a long way off. Oz just had that kind of effect. "Why don't you go grab a pizza with the guys and I'll talk to you later."

"You sure you don't need me to come by?"

"I'm sure." Willow told him good-bye and punched the phone off. She stood by the window looking out into the garden. The moonlight barely broke the darkness. *Buffy's out there, somewhere, doing her thang. The least I can do is handle my own baby-sitting and lobbying job.* She folded her arms across her chest, feeling the chill that suddenly raced through her despite the fuzzy sweater she wore against the night chill.

She returned to the couch and tried to get interested in the book again. It was no use. Her famed powers of concentration were shaken. *Fear, the number-one cause of dyslexia.*

Her attention focused on the intercom again. Something still bothered her about it. She flipped the toggle, opening the channel to the baby's room.

She heard nothing.

Flipping the switch off, she tried to relax. She was in mid-sip of the diet soda that was going steadily flatter when she realized what was bothering her about the intercom. She flipped it on again.

She heard *nothing*. And nothing wasn't a good thing to hear.

She didn't hear Baby Tad snoring either. Nothing sounded at the other end of the transmission. A cold ball of fear formed in Willow's stomach as she grabbed the cordless phone and raced toward the staircase leading to the second floor.

Visions of the shuttered window by the baby's bed

formed in her mind. *Please don't let the bumps have been the sound of the windows slamming against the house!*

She punched Oz's number into the phone. It started ringing as she reached the stairs. Before she got halfway up, all the lights in the house went out and darkness settled in around Willow.

CHAPTER 2

Buffy reloaded the crossbow on the run. *Now there's dexterity!* Glancing over her shoulder, she saw at least six vampires coming after them. Gaining ground in fact. . . .

"Which way?" Giles asked breathlessly.

Sprinting quickly to the side, Buffy glanced ahead. Yellow earth-moving monster machines occupied the clearing ahead. She recognized bulldozers and backhoes and other tracked vehicles designed to rip, dig, or shove the earth.

"The equipment," she told Giles. "It's bigger than the trees. It'll give us more cover."

The Watcher ran for the nearest bulldozer.

I never should have let him come out here, Buffy chided herself. *I knew the forest was starting to fill up with these guys.* She and Xander had stopped in at

Willy's tavern only yesterday and found out about the gathering of vamps at the forest.

Giles ducked under the bulldozer. He hunkered down and glanced at her. "Come on, Buffy!"

"Do me a favor," Buffy said. "Just stay there a minute and keep out of the way." She didn't mean it in a bad way, but they both knew she was better than him at this sort of thing. It was kind of what made him the Watcher and her the Slayer. Watchers watched, and Slayers slayed.

Not breaking stride, Buffy launched herself into the air. She turned a complete somersault in the air and landed on top of the bulldozer's engine cowling facing the direction she'd come from.

The lead vampire had been an older female before she'd died and come back. Her gray hair flared out behind her, proof that a bad hair day could come back to haunt someone. Her yellow fangs glinted in the moonlight, and a silvery bubble of anxious saliva gleamed on her lips.

Buffy aimed the crossbow and put the shaft through her heart. The creature stopped for just a moment, then exploded into a shower of ash that the two vampires behind her rushed through without slowing down.

Dropping the crossbow, Buffy reached into her backpack and pulled out a pair of wooden stakes. She twirled them in her hands and moved to counter the two young male vampires leaping up onto the bulldozer.

One of them landed in front of her while the other

dropped onto the canopy over the operator's seat. "Stakes?" the one in front of her asked.

"Well, I've done the Shot-Through-the-Heart riff," Buffy said, "so I thought I'd try something a little more close up and personal." She feinted, then ducked to the left, drawing the young vampire in front of her out of his position.

He raked at her with his fingers, intending to rip her face off. Buffy dodged under the blow, taking a step behind him. Her Slayer senses also told her the vampire on the bulldozer's canopy was leaping down at her back as she turned.

Hooking her right elbow up into the first vampire's armpit and shoulder, Buffy flung him forward into the one that had leaped. They struck each other with a meaty impact, sounding like linemen in a football game. Before they could disentangle from each other, she staked the one she'd thrown.

The vampire disintegrated, falling to ashes at her feet. "Oh man," the other vampire said, backing away. He tried to leap up onto the bulldozer's canopy again.

Buffy threw herself after him. She grabbed him by the shirt collar with her free hand. They fell over the side and crashed to the ground. The fall dazed Buffy for just a moment, but she recovered quickly. She pushed herself up and started to stake her quarry. Then she noticed one of the other vampires dragging Giles from under the bulldozer.

The librarian fought back valiantly, punching and kicking, but the blows had no effect on the creature that held him. The vamp grinned, revealing huge canines.

"Giles!" Buffy called. He turned and she tossed the stake to him underhanded.

Giles caught the stake, then shoved the sharp point toward the vampire who hissed and jumped back. "Thank you," the Watcher said over his shoulder. "I'll be back in a moment." He took a better grip on the stake and pursued the vampire.

Buffy's attention returned to the vampire she confronted.

"Lost your toothpick," the vampire taunted. He stood and came at her.

Holding her hands in front of her, Buffy straight-armed him in the forehead, snapping his head back. She whirled and sidestepped, bringing a slashing backfist into the vampire's mouth. His fangs shattered with loud pops. "That comes from not flossing between kills," Buffy said.

The vampire clapped a hand over his mouth and howled in disbelief. "Ou mroke muh teef! Ou mroke muh teef!" He sank to the ground, momentarily stunned.

A shadow slipped across the ground to Buffy's right. Without hesitating the Slayer leaped straight up and flipped over, coming down with her heels on the back of another vampire. She drove the creature to the ground.

In her life, this vampire had been a girl not much older than Buffy. She howled in rage and rolled over, raking out a handful of sharp talons.

Buffy flipped again, already knowing the direction she needed to move. A half-dozen two-by-fours lay on the ground near the bulldozer. She landed and picked the end of one up while the girl vamp hurled herself forward again.

Stamping on the middle of the two-by-four, Buffy cracked it. She picked up the three-foot section she held, satisfied with the irregular edge the break had created. She rammed it into the attacking vampire.

Ashes fell where the creature had once stood.

Buffy braced herself and threw the other section of the wood at the vampire whose teeth she'd broken. He exploded when the jagged end pierced his heart.

Glancing toward Giles, Buffy saw the librarian had managed to stake the creature that had attacked him. She gave him a smile, then retreated to her backpack while the remaining two vampires tried to figure out what they wanted to do. She grabbed two more stakes from the backpack. What good is a Slayer who doesn't accessorize to the max?

The vampires broke and ran, plunging into the forest.

"Well," Giles said, "that was exciting."

Buffy tossed him one of the stakes. "Oh, we're not done yet." She took up the chase.

Willow stumbled on the stairs in the darkness. She grabbed the railing, listening to the phone ring and ring in her ear. Panic welled up inside her, tightening her breath. She made herself be calm. Realizing that Oz and the band must have already gone for pizza and no one was there, she punched the phone off.

Oz's gone. Buffy's gone. Xander! Gotta be Xander! She punched Xander's number on the phone's lighted keypad. Cupping it to her ear again, she started up the stairs again. *Tad's up there! I hope!*

It almost broke Willow's heart to think of the baby lying up in his bed alone and unprotected. At the top of the stairs she searched the wall with her free hand and found the rechargeable flashlight hanging there.

The phone picked up. "Hi, this is Xander's machine," Xander's voice said. "Xander's not here right now. Leave your name and number at the beep."

Willow beat the beep and punched the phone off. She switched on the flashlight and a cone of yellow illumination splashed against the ceiling. She adjusted it, pointing it toward the baby's room. The door remained closed.

Okay, okay, be calm, Will, be calm. . . .

At the end of the hallway, a window overlooked the upwardly mobile residential area. Lights glowed in all the other houses.

Not good, she told herself. *It's not good to be the only house without lights.* She looked around for a weapon, then realized she was all out of hands. *Phone, flashlight. It's a start.* She crept across the smooth wooden floor that, thankfully, didn't creak underfoot.

She listened at the door and heard nothing. She'd already decided that was bad. Thinking maybe Xander was over at Cordelia's, she punched in that number.

"Hello?" Cordelia said. "I don't recognize the name or number showing on my Caller ID, so this had better not be a prank call. I'll track you down and—"

"Cordelia," Willow whispered hoarsely, "it's me." She hated that she was reduced to asking Cordelia for help.

"I see," Cordelia said, clearly not seeing. "Is this Me Smith or Me Jones? I get you two confused sometimes."

Willow put a trembling hand on the door, not liking what her mind was conjuring up about the baby. *Xander Harris, you're going to pay for all those movies you dragged me to.* "Cordelia, it's Willow."

"Willow? You sound like you have a cold."

"I'm whispering because I don't want to be heard." Willow put her hand on the doorknob and turned. It turned easily. That was good. Or maybe it was bad.

"If you don't want to be heard, why are you calling?"

"Something's here with me." Willow pushed the door inward slightly and peered through the crack. She barely saw the baby bed. The window on the other side of the room appeared closed and intact. She felt a little better.

"Something as in fanged and gruesome?"

"I don't know. I'm over at the Campbells' house baby-sitting."

"Baby-sitting?" Cordelia made it sound like leprosy.

"It was a favor."

"Isn't there a Campbell on the zoning commission over the park development?" Cordelia's tone turned suspicious.

Cordelia's knowledge of that surprised Willow. Usually Cordelia showed more interest in fashion and hairstyles. And heading up the planning committee for the Spring Blow-Out. "Yes, but—"

Cordelia shifted into outrage. "You went there to talk about Gallivan Industries and the amusement park?"

"No. They asked me to baby-sit. I was going to talk to him later."

"Willow, this is so beneath you! I can't believe—"

"Cordelia, shut up and listen." Willow gasped, feeling guilty and totally weirded out as she stepped into the baby's room. Nothing moved. *Please let the baby be asleep.* She crept toward the crib on trembling legs. "I'm over here and something's going on. I heard these noises, like somebody might have been climbing on the roof."

"Probably a cat," Cordelia said. "Do they have a cat?"

"No. But the lights are out."

"Power outages happen all the time."

Give it up, Will, she thought. *Cordy's no help.* Willow forced herself to take a deep breath. "I was calling to see if Xander was there."

"No. He's out with his new best bud, Hutch, at the mall. They're coloring comics or something." Cordelia sounded put out. "And I really don't appreciate the way you're handling this. You and your pathetic Greenpeace wannabes could really endanger our chances of having the Spring Blow-Out. If Gallivan gets upset, he'll ban us from the park. And might I remind you that most of the student body stands with me in thinking that is oh-so uncool?"

"This isn't a power outage," Willow said. "This house is the only one affected. Every other house has their lights on."

"So a breaker broke or a fuse fizzled. What's the diff? You're in the dark, right? I find that very symbolic."

"I'm worried about what's in the dark with me." Willow stopped at the edge of the baby bed.

"Your imagination," Cordelia responded. "It's lurking everywhere. You're frazzled. You need a party. You should lay off protesting Gallivan Industries till after the Spring Blow-Out."

"That's on Friday," Willow said automatically. "They're voting on the rezoning on Thursday. By Friday it would be too late to do anything."

"Whatever. Look, I've really got to be going now. Lots of plans to make, lots of people to call. They're going to be talking about this Spring Blow-Out for years."

"Don't you dare hang up yet," Willow said. She tracked the flashlight up toward the baby.

"What?" Cordelia asked in disbelief.

The flashlight spilled light into the baby bed, reflecting from the white paint. The baby looked small under the covers. Tad was only eight months old. He still slept on his stomach with his butt pushed up into the air. One small fist rested at his mouth.

"What did you just tell me?" Cordelia hissed.

Willow released a pent-up breath she hadn't known she'd been holding. She couldn't believe she'd been so forceful with Cordelia. "Look," she whispered into the phone, "I'm sorry. But with all the noise and all those awful movies Xander used to take me to, I guess I was kind of out of line."

"Out of line?" Cordelia snapped. "You were off the map!"

Willow got a little angry, and it felt kind of good after being so scared. It was good that the baby was safe, but she still didn't know why the power was off. She played the flashlight over the rest of the room, checking it out. "Hey, I apologized. I—"

"Willow!"

Goosebumps crawled onto Willow's neck when she heard the cold, raspy voice echo in the quietness of the room.

"An apology isn't acceptable," Cordelia was saying in her other ear. "Just because I hang out with Buffy and you guys staking the occasional vampire and whatever would-be monster or ancient curse that happens to come along doesn't mean we're anywhere near the same social level. You—"

Willow turned back to the crib. The flashlight beam played over Baby Tad.

He was sitting up, his little round head now too big for his body. He looked like an unfinished sculpture, kind of soft and doughy around the edges, the way all babies did. He wore a Mickey Mouse sleeper. But his eyes glowed hot green like molten jade. A look of pure evil filled them.

"Willow," Tad said again, milky drool trickling down the side of his chin. "We need to talk."

CHAPTER 3

Whoops! Looks like I just made the Buffy-et line!
Buffy spotted the ambush too late to stop. The two
vampires she had been following charged her from
both sides, leaping at her in snarling fury.

She continued on another step, then put on the
brakes. Her boots bit into the soft earth, skidding for
just a moment.

Unable to stop themselves in their headlong
plunges, the vampires slammed into each other.
They went down in a tangle of arms and legs. Both of
them were young men hardly older than Buffy. They
wore prep school clothing, letting Buffy know whoever had sired them had been hunting in the areas
near the private school.

She drove her stake through the heart of the first
one. He turned to a pile of dust in a heartbeat, his
scream dying in mid-protest.

The other vampire, sallow and thin, with a bad case of acne showing across the vampiric distortions on his face, tried to get to his feet.

Buffy stepped forward and roundhouse kicked him in the chest, sprawling him onto the ground again. Huffing, Giles came up behind him. The Watcher raised the stake.

"Wait!" the vampire begged. "Don't kill me! I haven't even bitten anybody! This is my first night!"

Giles stopped, panting hoarsely.

Buffy strode over to the vampire, who tried to get up. She lightly kicked the top of his head, bouncing his head back. "Stay down. I want to know what you're doing here."

The vampire hesitated.

"Come on, come on," Buffy said irritably. "This isn't hard. You ever see *Dragnet?*"

The vampire looked at her with his bloodshot eyes. "Is that some kind of Vegas show thing? 'Cause if it is, I was never into that kind of stuff."

"Dragnet," Buffy repeated. "Kind of an early *NYPD Blue.* Heavy into questions and answers. You get to play along. I ask, you answer."

"Or you'll slap me on the head?"

"Or I'll stake you like a butterfly in biology class," Buffy promised. *It's hard to pull off the little-lost-boy look with a face only a mommy vampire could love.*

The vampire kid shrugged nervously. "Okay."

Buffy simultaneously kept watch over the darkness around them. She didn't for an instant believe all the vamps in the immediate vicinity had been dealt with. "What are you doing here?"

"I was with Brandon. The guy you staked. He told me there was something big going on here."

"What kind of big?"

"I don't know. I just crawled out of my grave. This is all still kind of new to me." The vampire looked at Buffy, then at Giles, as if seeking some kind of empathy. "I mean, you see the movies and stuff, but man," he shook his head, "it really just doesn't prepare you for this whole vampire gig, you know."

"Big," Buffy reminded.

"Supposed to be some kind of group thing down here. I got the impression they were looking for something. From the way Brandon was talking about it, I figured it must be pretty intense."

Buffy tried another tack. "Did he say anything about Gallivan Industries?"

"Who're they?"

Okay, we're on to the next topic. "Sunnydale High's Spring Blow-Out?"

The vampire grinned. "Sounds cool. When's it going to be?"

Buffy shot him a disapproving look.

The grin died. "I guess you probably wouldn't appreciate party-crashers, huh?"

Buffy showed him an evil smile. "A vampire party-crasher? Sure. Add a stake and they're more fun than a piñata."

"I'll take it off my to-do list."

"Fantastic. What are they looking for?"

"I told you I didn't know," the vampire protested.

"Is it a person?" Giles spoke up now. "Or is it something in the ground?"

The vampire looked uneasy. "I'm going to have to guess here."

"I'll take Guessing for two hundred, Alex," Buffy said.

The vampire nodded. "A few of them brought shovels."

Buffy looked at Giles. "Treasure hunt?"

"Actually," the Watcher replied, "there's an archeological dig site in these woods that I've heard about."

"You'd have figured the news would have covered it," Buffy replied.

"The amusement park Gallivan Industries is proposing took precedence. It was an early American Indian fishing village," Giles said. "Some of the professors and students at university here were participating in it."

Buffy shifted her attention back to the vampire. "Were they digging up stuff from the archeological site?"

"I never saw anything like that. But we just got here a little while ago. Maybe we missed it."

"It's supposed to be a little further on," Giles said.

"And you know this how?" Buffy asked.

"Pathfinder?" Giles tried.

Buffy rolled her eyes.

Giles cleared his throat. "The papers had a map. I'm sure it'll be clearly marked, and very noticeable if it isn't. The university managed to get a court injunction against Gallivan rooting around in that area until they're able to finish excavating the area."

"Then we go check out the dig site," Buffy said.

"Cool," the vampire said, getting to his feet slowly. "Then everybody's happy? I can go?"

Buffy swung too quickly for the creature to compensate, burying the stake into his chest and driving it into the heart beyond.

He opened his mouth to scream but turned into a shower of falling dust.

"He's gone," Buffy said, feeling only a little bad about what she'd done. The vampire had been a human being at one time. *Maybe he'd been a good one and maybe not. But the thing was, he wasn't human anymore.* "And so are we. Which way is this dig thingy?"

Willow tried to speak but couldn't.

Baby Tad glared at her with that impossible molten jade stare. *"Willow, why haven't you worked harder to protect the forest?"* he asked in his hoarse, raspy voice.

Finally, she got her legs to work. She took two steps backward. *Not ideal for baby's first words.*

Grimacing, the baby jumped up in the bed and grabbed the railing. *"No! You won't be allowed to get away so easily."* The creature gestured with a tiny fist.

Abruptly, the door behind Willow slammed shut, sounding like a cannon going off in the small room. Hands shaking, her mind racing, she almost dropped the flashlight. She forced her voice to work. "Where's the baby?"

"Willow," it rasped, *"you believe in our cause."*

"What cause?" Willow asked. "I don't know what you're talking about." She held the flashlight trained on the creature in the baby bed. Creature, monster—it definitely wasn't a baby.

"You've fought against the transgressor Hector Gallivan," the creature said. Its voice, in spite of the hoarse raspiness, held a plaintive whine. *"You must champion the forest. It must not fall to his cruel blades, to the smoke-snorting foul beasts that run on tracks which even now sleep in our forest. You must help us bring the Homestone back so that we can take our proper place."*

"Gallivan?" Willow repeated. *Homestone?*

"Gallivan?" Cordelia's voice came out of the air. "Did you say Gallivan?"

Suddenly remembering the cordless phone in her hand, Willow clapped it to the side of her face. "Cordelia?"

"What's going on over there?" Cordelia demanded.

"It's the baby," Willow whispered. "I mean, it can't *be* the baby, but it *looks* like the baby. Whatever it is. Cordelia, I need help. Get Xander over here. Buffy's not at home and I can't reach Oz."

"We thought you believed, Willow," the thing in the baby bed told her. *"You have your powers. They bind you more to the natural world than most humans."*

Willow continued backing away, trying to take

small steps so the thing wouldn't notice. *Small step, he can't see you . . . small step, he can't see you . . . small step . . .*

"Willow," Cordelia warned, "this had better not be some kind of trick."

"I don't play gags, remember? I've been the punch line all my life." Willow kept the flashlight shining in the molten jade eyes, hoping the brightness interfered with its vision. "This is me, Willow. I can't help but tell the truth. And the truth is that a monster has taken over Tad's body."

"Big sigh," Cordelia said with exaggeration. "I need an address."

Desperation. That's the only reason I'm not hanging up on her right now. Willow repeated the address three times till she got it right.

"Don't go away, Willow," the thing pleaded. "Many will be harmed if you refuse to act. The Homestone must be made."

"Who's going to be harmed?" *Besides maybe me.* Willow wished she could grow another arm to try the doorknob. *Flashlight, phone. Flashlight, phone. Which can I do without?*

"Anyone who stands against us," the creature said, shifting agitatedly on the other side of the crib railing. "We-of-Shadows will be hurt if they can't stop the Gallivan transgressor."

"What are you talking about?" Willow asked.

The creature thrust out a small fist again.

Without warning, the cordless phone spat out a series of violet sparks. *Lost the baby, broke the phone. This is not a stellar evening.* Willow dropped the dead handset and reached for the doorknob. It refused to budge.

"You must help us, Willow," the creature said. *"Your work to save the park and the forest has not escaped notice of your own kind and ours."*

"What work?" Willow asked, her mind struggling to make the necessary connections. "The protests we've done at Weatherly Park?" There'd only been two of them so far, both of them kind of pathetic actually. But they had attracted the attention of the local media, which planned to do a feature on the protest she'd organized for Wednesday.

"You're fighting the fight of We-of-Shadows," the creature said. *"We wanted to acknowledge your efforts."*

"By possessing the baby I was sent here to take care of?" Willow asked. "Trust me, that's not really a good plan. A card would have been fine."

"We thought perhaps we could help."

Willow drew in a breath, growing a little more brave thinking about the baby rather than herself. "What did you do with Tad?"

The thing gazed at her. *"What was necessary."*

Doesn't sound good. Different tack. "How did you know I was going to be here?"

"I didn't. It was merely good fortune. Yours, and ours. You have power as a witch, Willow. We can help you learn more about that power."

"Reality check. I want you to release Tad," Willow said.

A hint of sadness darkened the creature's face. *"I can't do that. Campbell must see the error of his support of Hector Gallivan. The forest must not be made to suffer."*

Willow thought frantically. It would have been so much better if Buffy was here. Buffy had no problem about knowing what to do—even when she didn't know what to do.

Another door to the side of the crib led to a small bathroom. She'd been in it earlier when she'd changed Tad. *At least, I hope that was Tad!* Cautiously, she made her way to the door.

"You must join us, Willow. We can give you the power you need to prevent the cursed mechanical beasts from ravaging the forest." The creature turned its baby-sized head in her direction. *"Where are you going?"*

Willow darted forward even as the creature raised its hand. The scent inside the bathroom told her she'd been right. The potpourri bound up in the little straw basket sitting on the sink area included bayberry leaves.

"Willow!" Working quickly, Willow grabbed the potpourri basket and emptied it into her hand. The moonlight streaming through the window created barely enough illumination to see by, but she sorted through the herbs. Since she'd started studying witchcraft, she'd learned a lot more than the life science teachers had ever thought about teaching her.

"Willow!" The railing on the baby bed rattled furiously. *"What are you doing, Willow?"*

Separating the bayberry leaves out from the other herbs, Willow reduced the pile to a pinch she could hold between her thumb and forefinger. *I hope this is enough.* She walked back toward the creature in Tad's body. Her heart pounded in her chest. "I . . . I had to get something," she said.

The creature's nose wrinkled and it sneezed. It was a perfect, baby-sounding sneeze, hardly louder than a cat's. *"What?"* it asked petulantly. It clung to the railing with both small fists. Innocence glowed in its eyes.

Willow crushed the bayberry leaves between her thumb and forefinger. Then she sprinkled them onto the creature. "Bayberry leaves," she said. "And if you know your spellcraft as much as you think you do, you'll know that witches use it to break demonic possession."

The bayberry leaves floated down onto the creature. It snarled in pain and spat angrily. *"I'm no demon!"* it shouted. *"No common flesh stealer or mind waster! I am of We-of-Shadows, of the forest!"* Where the bayberry leaves touched it, the creature's baby-soft skin erupted in huge blisters.

Willow dodged back as it flailed at her.

"Filthy human witch!" it growled. *"We should have known better than to trust you!"*

Willow watched, hypnotized, as the bayberry leaves continued to sizzle against the tender flesh. The herb melted away, puddling at the creature's feet. It threw its head back and howled again, and olive-colored skin showed under the baby-pink texture. Two of the bigger blisters on its back suddenly exploded, releasing a pair of gossamer wings that looked sleek and shiny as they caught the moonlight.

The creature's features morphed into a twisted, knotted grimace of pain and rage. Its hands and feet morphed as well, growing longer and slimmer, equipped with razor-sharp curved talons that shredded the bedsheets. With a cry of rage, it reached down into the bed and picked up a small, razor-sharp axe. It leaped up into the air, beat the gossamer wings, and sped straight at Willow.

This, Willow thought, *this is definitely not good.*

CHAPTER 4

*B*uffy hunkered down in the shadows on top of the hill overlooking the dig site. Red flags with the seal of the local university jutted up from the ground on wire spindles around the excavation site. Mounds of dirt stood in tall cones. Even the air smelled dirty. *Terrific. Rooting around in an overgrown anthill just tops off the evening.*

"Well, they've been busy," Giles stated.

Buffy nodded. She scanned the forest and the scarred earth in an effort to spot any of the other vampires possibly prowling the area. She took the broken branches she'd scavenged along the way from her pockets and dropped them onto the ground. She worked them quickly into shape, shaving them to crooked points with the lock-back knife she carried. She still couldn't get the Willow and Cordy situation off her mind. "You're right about the Blow-Out."

"Oh?"

"Yeah. Things are kind of tense between Willow and Cordelia right now over the Spring Blow-Out." Buffy kept peeling splinters from the branches, adding a third one to the two she'd already sharpened, then reaching for a fourth. "Everybody's ready to party, but Willow's really wigging out over losing Weatherly Park. She grew up here. It means something to her. And then there's this whole environmental issue thing."

"She's taking a decidedly more conservational approach to things since she became a witch."

"It's getting in the way of the party."

"And that's what it boils down to for you?"

Not exactly, but it's in the ballpark. Buffy felt guilty for just a moment. "If Gallivan Industries puts the amusement park in, it'll add about four hundred jobs to the community. Some of those will be summer jobs for people my age." *There, that was something positive.*

"That's one of the advantages Gallivan Industries has mentioned to the press, I believe," Giles said.

"The additional draw created by the amusement park will also help the local businesses," Buffy pointed out.

"That's another of Gallivan's arguments." Giles looked at her in that totally Watcher way he had of his that sometimes put Buffy so on edge. "So do you support your friend, or do you—eh, party?"

"It's not that simple," Buffy said. *But it sure stacks up into an either-or pretty quick.* "Cordy's heading up the Spring Blow-Out organizational committee."

"Yes," Giles said, "but I think we can agree that even at the best of times, your relationship with Cordelia Chase isn't necessarily the best."

Buffy reached for another branch. She felt tired and bruised from fighting the vampires. Luckily, with her Slayer's enhanced constitution, she'd be virtually unmarked by morning. Giles wasn't so fortunate; he'd be hurting for days.

"No," Buffy said quietly, "if I had to pick between them, I'd pick Willow."

"Except that you haven't."

"There's still what *I* want to consider. And there's Xander."

"Ah yes, Xander. Where does he fit in?"

"Xander is Willow's friend and has been for a long time," Buffy replied. "But he's also now Cordelia's boyfriend. You can do the math on that one."

"He's going to be somewhat conflicted."

"More than likely he's going to side with Cordelia."

"Leaving poor Willow to carry on alone."

Poor Willow? Oh, now that's heaping on the guilt. "Yeah, and that kind of flat-lines the warm fuzzy I'm supposed to get when I think of the party."

"I see. However, that doesn't tell me how you feel."

"Confused," Buffy admitted. "Slaying's much easier. Find the vamps, stake 'em, and move on."

"Except slaying isn't all you have to do."

"No. What I'm doing out here tonight is trying to clear the decks for the Blow-Out. *If* it happens. As I told you, I was patrolling the funeral homes and what do I find but one of the workmen who was killed out here today rising up out of his coffin." That was when she'd called Giles in.

"I recall reading about the death in the paper. I thought the workman was electrocuted."

"That's what the news story said," Buffy agreed. "Maybe it even looked that way. But the medical examiner missed the big absence of blood. We've already noticed how they do that around here, though, so no big surprise. Anyway, the guy rose up and we chatted."

"Only in the early stages, they're sometimes not too communicative," Giles said, remembering.

"And about as friendly as the lunch ladies in the cafeteria during a health department inspection." Buffy gathered her stakes. "He didn't have much to say, but I knew there was a problem. I started wondering how involved Gallivan is."

"You're suspicious of him?" Giles asked.

"Gallivan was sanctioned by the mayor, and it was one of his workmen who got taken out at night. After they were supposed to be off for the night. I also didn't know about the dig."

"Yes, well, those two items shouldn't be connected."

"Then again." Buffy pointed at the trio of shadows that moved out from the treeline and walked toward the dig. Their skin was pasty white under the pale moonlight, and their faces held the bumpy look of vampires. Two of them carried shovels while the third carried a pick.

"Interesting," Giles murmured, lowering his voice.

"Dangerous," Buffy said. "If the vampires are still lurking the night of the Spring Blow-Out they're going to have a chance at a lot of victims. I can't let that happen." She crept down the incline, staying hidden among the trees.

Giles moved quietly behind her.

"The vampires I figure I can handle," Buffy said. "The problem's going to be how to deal with Willow and Cordelia. That makes refereeing a *Springer* show look easy." She kept going, dropping into full Slayer mode as she closed on her prey.

Cordelia Chase put her foot down on the accelerator and burned through a traffic light just as it turned red. She checked her image in the rearview mirror. She was tall and had a figure that was to die for. Most of it was simply good genes and being unafraid of a total commitment to the Look.

She'd pulled her dark hair back in case Willow's call resulted in some real Slayage, and she wore a cerise turtleneck, a hip-hugging black Spandex mini, and high black boots. Power colors. She'd even grabbed three pairs of earrings on her way out the door. Getting the right pair selected and on was tricky while driving like she was late for the checkered flag at the Indianapolis 500, but not impossible. Looking good was never impossible for Cordelia. Never would be.

Cordelia pulled hard on the wheel, and punched her cell phone's keypad. She narrowly avoided a sports utility vehicle with a Pizza Delivery sign on it. She had to check her rearview mirror to make sure she'd really seen that. *Très gauche,* she thought with a shudder. *Or the tips are really good. Nah. The tips will never be that good.*

There was still no answer at the Campbells' house. She punched the end button and tried another number.

"Out of This World Comics," a cheery voice said. "If you're leaving the solar system, let us help you pack."

"Is Xander Harris there?" Cordelia asked.

"Xander? He was a minute ago. Oh, there he is. Hang on." The phone bumped and rattled, and the connection faded in and out.

Cordelia made a right turn, screeching around the corner. *Why couldn't Buffy be here? She's never around when you need her.* She roared around another corner, still waiting, and felt a familiar sickening crunch. Fearfully, she glanced at her steering hand, straightening her fingers out slowly in denial. When she saw the broken nail, she wanted to scream.

"Hey," Xander greeted her.

"What are you doing there?" Cordelia demanded.

"Hanging with Hutch," Xander answered somewhat sullenly. "You were busy with the Spring Blow-Out committee, remember?" Hutch worked at the Out of This World Comics shop in the mall. Xander had developed a friendship with the guy because they shared a lot of the same interests. They were interests that Cordelia would never have.

And Hutch kind of creeped her out. She'd never

seen anybody eat as much as he did and never gain an ounce. He also had a more morbid and whacked sense of humor than Xander, and didn't mind if his remarks hurt people.

"I remember you weren't interested in helping." Cordelia eyed the broken nail ruefully. *If Willow's not in trouble, and I mean the blood-spurting kind, she's going to need physical therapy to walk again.*

"Sure I was," Xander replied. "Up until the point where your answers to my suggestions went from 'I don't think so' to 'That's just stupid.' Then, as I recall, I took my leave and you weren't unhappy to see me go."

"Well, if you'd hung around you could be answering this call for help instead of me," Cordelia said.

"Who's calling for help?" he asked shifting from the lighthearted banter to full-blown seriousness. Most people missed that quality in him, that ability to go from carefree to concerned. Of course, the annoying thing to Cordelia was that *she* couldn't control it. "Buffy?"

"Willow," Cordelia said. "She's baby-sitting at the Campbells' and called to tell me the baby turned into some kind of monster."

"Did she say what kind?"

"She didn't have time. The phone went dead."

"Is Willow okay?"

Cordelia heard the concern in Xander's voice and it grated on her nerves. True, Xander and Willow had a friendship that went back to a time when they were kids, but he was going to have to put that behind him sometime. Or at least, tone it down a bit around her. *There are, after all, my feelings to consider.* "I don't know. I'm on my way over there now," she replied as icily as possible. "But, just in case, I thought I'd call you and let you know."

"I'm gone," Xander promised. His voice rose as he turned away from the phone. "Hutch! Hey, man, can you give me a lift somewhere? I've got your gas covered." He turned back to the phone, his voice clearer. "I'm on my way, Cordy. Be careful till I get there."

"If I was going to be careful, I'd have stayed home. I broke a nail." Cordelia punched the end button and dropped the phone onto the passenger seat.

Willow ducked and covered her head to avoid the initial attack. She swung the flashlight wildly in the direction of the flying creature, which still looked a little like the baby despite the changes. She missed, and thankfully it did too.

She pushed up out of her crouch and sprinted for the door. Gripping the knob, she discovered it took effort to open it, but the door did open. She fled through just as the heavy buzz of the gossamer wings' beating closed in on her.

"Willow!" it cried out in anger and pain behind her.

Something thumped into the door and she glanced back to see what it was. The axehead, no bigger than her palm, jutted out of the splintered wood of the door.

It means business! she thought. She whirled around and raced for the stairway, grabbing the corner post and wheeling around to descend the steps in a loud clatter.

The bedroom door gusted open behind her, slamming into the wall. Halfway down the steps, she glanced up and saw the flying creature in immediate pursuit.

Willow ran down the stairs, barely managing to stay upright with one hand on the banister. Her breath came in choked gasps even though she tried to make herself stay calm. *Calm? Calm doesn't mix with trying to set a new Olympic record.* She ran across the living room, through the foyer, and to the front door. She yanked on the door, but it held fast. Reversing direction, she abandoned the door and raced for the kitchen.

The heavy buzz of the gossamer wings beat the air frantically after her.

Willow sped around the corner and nearly slipped on the waxed sheen of the hardwood floor. She flung out a hand against the wall and regained her balance, zigzagging around the heavy kitchen island in front of her. Pots and pans hanging over the counter caught the outside illumination and their flat surfaces glittered like a collection of miniature moons.

She flung open the heavy drapes covering the sliding glass door that led to the outside patio, her fingers clawing at the latch . . .

CHAPTER 5

The patio doors wouldn't open. Chest heaving with fear, all out of places to run, Willow glanced around the kitchen, then settled on the hanging pots and pans. She edged over to them, keeping the tiled counter to her back.

The winged creature stayed several feet away, hovering like a bumblebee. The drone of its wings filled the kitchen.

Working on adrenaline and anger, Willow darted forward, reaching toward the pots above the counter even as she saw the creature dart forward. She seized a large frying pan, gripping the long handle in both fists. Still moving, knowing everything depended on speed, she swung the heavy pan at the creature.

The flying creature flapped its gleaming wings harder and rose above the swing. The pan *whooshed* by, missing only by inches.

The momentum carried Willow around hard enough to crack tile from the counter. Chips sprayed the wall. She turned back around, her hair flying into her eyes.

"You will join us, Willow. When the time is right." The creature drew a gnarled hand from the small leather pouch at its side. Gleaming sparkles rained through the air like a miniature radioactive dust cloud.

Dust to dust? It wasn't a cheery thought. Willow tried to avoid it but couldn't. She tried to hold her breath, but that wasn't possible either. The dust swirled around her head when she breathed in. *Yuck! What was that?* She had a brief impression of the hardwood floor coming up to meet her, and then she didn't know anything. Her last thought was about Tad. *Where's the* real *baby?*

Buffy crept to the edge of the excavation site and looked down at the three vampires digging into the soft black earth. They'd spread out, chopping into the ground in different places.

"Anybody know what this thing is supposed to look like?" a vampire dressed in a tennis outfit asked. In real life he'd probably have been a middle-aged stockbroker or an insurance agent.

"Hey Grandpa, Dad wants to know if we know what we're looking for," a younger vampire in skateboard gear said.

"If we knew," the third vampire said, stepping on his shovel to drive it deeper, "everybody would probably know. It'd be gone by now." He had been an old man in his last life, dressed in Bermuda shorts with high black socks and a wrinkled fishing hat.

"Yeah," the young vampire snarled, "but we could always take it from them."

"That's your answer to everything, isn't it?" the father vampire asked irritably. "Just take it."

"Hey, Dad, get a clue. We're kind of dead now, and when me and Gramps bring up a victim, I don't see you turning it away. They aren't exactly *giving* their blood away, remember? At least, I think that's what all that kicking and screaming is about." He cackled maniacally as a sharp crack sounded from the earth. "Hey, I found a skeleton." He yanked it from the loose earth and scanned it. Obviously not finding anything that interested him, he tossed it aside and went back to digging.

The father vampire ignored him. "Think about it. If we're digging in the right place, why aren't the others here digging too?"

The grandpa vampire turned around. "That's what's wrong with your generation. All you want to do is sit around and whine about how hard you got it. At least your son is willing to get out there and fight for what he wants instead of sitting back and getting therapy to understand his needs."

Dysfunctional in life, dysfunctional in death. Family therapy will no longer help you, Buffy thought. Knowing it wasn't going to get any better and that she wasn't going to learn anything further, she stood up, stakes in both hands.

All three vampires turned toward her.

"I really hate to break up this Hallmark moment," she said, "but I've got a bone to pick with you."

The middle-aged man and his son retreated nervously.

The old vampire's face wrinkled in disgust. "Is that her?"

"Yeah, Grandpa," the youngest one said. "That's the Slayer."

The old vampire shook his head. "She don't look so tough."

"It's the bath oil beads," Buffy quipped. She moved with an economy of motion, stepping over the edge and dropping into the seven-foot pit.

The old vampire came at her first. He raised his pick and swung it, intending to drive it into Buffy's skull. Only she wasn't there when he got there. When he doubled over, following the pick blow, she drove a stake into his back, pushing it till it pierced his heart.

"Snot-nosed kids," the old vampire said, straightening to full height again. "Got no respect for your elders." He raised the pick again, but exploded into dust before he could begin the swing.

"Not when they go to pieces over the least little thing," Buffy said. She whirled to confront the remaining vampires.

The tennis player hurled his shovel at her. The edge gleamed for a split second in the moonlight.

Buffy sidestepped, then reached out and caught the shovel as it passed, stopping it in midflight. She lunged forward then, throwing it into the vampire's chest, rupturing the heart behind the breastbone as it drove through.

The skateboarder came at her, screaming and yelling. Claws and teeth seemed to be everywhere.

Holding a stake in each hand, Buffy used them like kama sticks to beat off each attack. She hit the boy's hands and feet, knocking them aside, and rained blows on his head till she staggered him. Setting herself, the Slayer spun and kicked him in the head, putting him back against the earthen wall. Before he could recover, she slammed a stake home in his chest.

"Yes, well . . . everything okay down there?" Giles asked.

"Yes." Buffy looked at the three piles of dust, then turned her attention to the excavation pit. "Have you ever worked on a dig, Giles?"

He clambered down into the pit to join her. "A few times. During grad school and for a short time thereafter. I did some volunteer work so I'd get a chance to see more of the world. I found it quite rewarding, actual—"

"Then tell me if you see anything interesting to vampires here." Buffy took a Maglite from her pants pocket and switched it on. The halogen bulb took away a lot of the shadows around them. Bright pits of metal shone against the dark earth.

"Well," Giles said, kneeling down, "they made a right and proper mess of it, didn't they?"

"I don't think archeology is a column in *Good Housekeeping*," Buffy said. She yawned, tired and grainy-eyed. She tried to remember there was a party that weekend. *Maybe*. She stayed at Giles's back, knowing he'd be totally absorbed in the clutter around him.

To Buffy the items he flicked through with his fingers just looked like bits of pottery, arrowheads, beads, a collection of bones deliberately shaped into some kind of tools. Nothing there held her interest, and she doubted it held any interest for the vampires either. *So why all the rooting around?* She hated puzzles presented by vampires. Puzzles and intrigues meant problems.

"This is an interesting dig," Giles said distractedly. His deft fingers pried still more objects from the ground. He brushed enough dirt off them to reveal what they were, then placed them on the ground. "But I don't think they're going to find anything out of the ordinary here."

"Yeah, but we've got vampires out here prowling through this. The Daily Double question is *why?*"

"Apparently that's the only noteworthy distinction this dig site is going to have about it." Giles scrambled to a different area and Buffy followed him with the light.

A crunching noise drew Buffy's attention. "Company," she whispered. She extinguished the Maglite.

Giles was half-focused on something he'd just

found, gazing at it intently. "More vampires?" he whispered.

Buffy jumped and pulled herself up to the edge of the pit, peering over. "Worse."

"What?"

Buffy studied the four men in uniform approaching the dig site. They had guns drawn and moved slowly. "Gallivan Industries security guards." She gazed at Giles. "Can't kill them and can't get caught."

He didn't respond, captivated by whatever he held in his hand.

"Giles," Buffy whispered, dropping back to his side, "correct me if I'm wrong, but I think this is the part where you tell me we need to get out of here."

"What?" He looked up at her, lost for only a moment. "Yes. Yes, we must get out of here."

"Any ideas?" Buffy heard the men's voices coming even closer. The security guards were almost on top of them.

Giles stood up, dodging the halogen flashlight beam that swept over the lip of the pit. "When we get the chance, run. Very fast."

Buffy stared at him in disbelief. "You went to Watcher school for that?"

Giles nudged the shovel on the ground with a foot. "I suppose we could always tunnel out." He gave her a small smile.

"If we were here with Bugs Bunny," Buffy replied. Footsteps crunched closer and more light poured into the excavation pit. *They're going to be on top of us any second,* the Slayer realized, *and my Watcher wants to play* Dig-Dug.

"Actually," Giles whispered. "I don't think old Bugs would be the answer either."

Buffy stared at him. "What?"

"Well," Giles stated quietly, "there's that wrong turn he was always taking at Albuquerque."

CHAPTER 6

A shiver of fear coursed through Cordelia as she crept toward the Campbell house. She'd found it easily enough with the address and Willow's directions. She left her car at the curb, the engine running in case they had to leave in a hurry.

She took a tense breath. *It's okay. If Willow can handle this, you can handle this. Only Willow's not handling, right? That's why she called.* Cordelia tried the front door but found it locked.

The privacy fence blocked the way at the side of the house. Muttering bad things about vampires in general and adding a few about Willow in particular, Cordelia climbed the privacy fence.

She'd gotten past the security guard at the gate to the development with a minimum of fuss by saying she was going to a party and didn't have the exact address. She'd told him she'd recognize the car, but it belonged to a real party guy who'd remember her. The security guard even had gone to the trouble of checking her story out, evidently having a short list of residents who regularly partied. He'd gotten the guy on the intercom and holding on to her license asked him if he knew Cordelia Chase.

The guy at the other end of the intercom had asked "Cordelia who?" *Clearly someone new to the area.* So Cordelia had stuck her head out and told him in her hottest voice, the one that Xander loved so much to hear over the phone, that they'd met at the Bronze and wouldn't he love to see her again?

The gates had opened in record time.

But if she got caught climbing the fence with a stake in her hand what was she—

"Hey, what's going on?"

Straddling the top of the fence, Cordelia glanced back down and saw Xander standing there. He was dark and lean, with a rebellious and mocking air that clung to him even before he let fly with the sarcastic comments that came to him so easily.

Hutch stood behind him. Cordelia tried to think of his last name and couldn't. She thought it started with a W. He was taller than Xander and heavier through the shoulders. His red hair was spiky. Earrings and two piercings above his left eyebrow gleamed in the moonlight. He wore khakis and a solid green collared pullover.

"I'm late for the Oklahoma Land Run," Cordelia said. "Tom Cruise was supposed to meet me there."

"I can see I've caught you at a bad time. Where's Willow?"

"She has to be inside. The front door's locked."

Xander nodded. He raised the lever on the gate and opened it. "Gate's not."

If he wasn't so worried about Willow, Cordelia knew he'd have laughed at her. Not long, because he also knew she wouldn't put up with it. "Get me down."

Xander reached up for her and helped her down inside the Campbells' yard.

"So what's the gig?" Hutch asked. His voice was smooth. *A natural singer's voice,* Cordelia thought.

"I don't know," she answered, leading the way through the flowers and shrubs to the redwood patio. "I just got here. How'd you get here so fast?"

"Hutch. Had to catch a ride from the mall, remember?" Xander jerked a thumb over his shoulder at his friend. "His family comes from a long line of moonshine runners. High speed to him is like shopping to you."

"Plus," Hutch said, "the mall's closer this way than the way you had to come."

"If I'd known you'd get here so fast," Cordelia said, "I'd have stayed home and you could have called me to let me know how everything turned out."

Xander ignored her.

She knew he was aware that some of the tough exterior she exhibited was false. A girl had to be tough if she was going to survive at or near the top of the heap. And Cordelia had her eye on the crown.

"Somebody has a floral fixation," Xander griped

in a whisper as they crept through the flowers, shrubs, and vines.

"There's nothing wrong with plants," Hutch said.

"Not in moderation." Xander paused at the patio's edge, then vaulted the railing, landing almost soundlessly.

"Somebody want to tell me why we're being so quiet?" Hutch asked. He linked his hands for Cordelia to step into.

Cordelia stepped into his hands and felt herself lifted easily. "Willow thought she heard a burglar."

"Any reason why she didn't call the security guards?" Hutch asked.

Cordelia looked at Xander, who managed to shrug while flattening himself beside the glass patio doors.

"Library fines?" Cordelia suggested. Hutch was busy climbing over the side of the elevated patio, trying not to make any noise.

"Right," Xander said, giving her a pained look. "Library fines. Late books, misuse of zealously guarded library property, double-checking in the reference section."

"Right," Hutch said. He glanced at the stake in Cordelia's hand. "Why are you carrying the stick?"

Cordelia looked at it. *Uh-oh.* "I found it."

"And thought it would make a family heirloom?"

"I was alone and there might have been a prowler. I didn't exactly find a laser gun lying around." *There's not much you can say to that,* she thought. She glanced at Xander, who was peering around the side of the door through the glass.

"Willow's on the floor in there!" Abandoning all

caution, he stepped in front of the door and reached for the handle. He yanked on the door, but it didn't open.

"Let me," Hutch said. When Xander stepped away, he gripped the handle and twisted. Muscles corded in his arm and the handle and the lock ripped away.

"Wow," Cordelia said. "Remind me not to shake hands with you. Ever."

Hutch tossed the handle and lock to the side. "Always been strong."

Xander pressed the glass door, rolling it back on its tracks with a bang. Cordelia followed him inside, covering his back. Xander knelt on the floor beside Willow and took her gently into his arms.

Watching them, Cordelia experienced a short but unpleasant pang of jealousy. Some days she didn't understand what attracted her to Xander, but other days she was envious of the time he'd spent with Willow and how closely they'd gotten to know each other. She sometimes wondered if she and Xander'd ever be that close, ever get past the boy-girl thing. Not that the boy-girl thing was bad, because it wasn't and she enjoyed it or she wouldn't have been there.

"Is she okay?" Cordelia glanced around the room, the stake tight in her fist, but she didn't see anything. *Of course, you don't always get to see it coming, do you?* The thought sent a shiver along her spine.

"She's coming around," Xander said. The note of relief in his voice irritated Cordelia at the same time it took away some of the worry about Willow.

Blinking and looking groggy, Willow peered up at

them. "The baby," she said. "I've got to find the baby." Suddenly frantic, she struggled to get to her feet but couldn't.

"Wait," Xander ordered. "I'll go check on the baby. Where is he?"

"That thing took him, Xander. I was supposed to watch him and I let him get taken away! It's all my fault!"

"Get ready to move," Buffy advised. "Fast." She scooped up a handful of loose dirt. "When this starts, you run back to the car. I'll catch up."

Reluctantly, the Watcher nodded. "On your mark, then."

The footsteps approached the edge of the excavation pit. Dirt and loose rock rained down over the side.

"Now!" Buffy said.

Giles broke and ran for the other side.

Stretching up, Buffy let fly with her handful of dirt. It smacked the security guard in the face, clouding his eyes.

"Help!" he yelled. "Over here!" He fired his pistol twice. Luckily, the bullets only killed tree branches.

Springing up, Buffy caught the edge of the excavation pit with her palms and pulled herself up. She threw a swinging leg block at the security guard and knocked him from his feet. As he fell, she plucked the pistol from his hand, broke open the cylinder and dumped the shells, then threw the weapon away. *One down, three to go.*

The other guards came on the run. Their flashlight

beams splashed against the dirt mounds, zipping across her too fast for them to get a lock on her. Gunshots rang out.

"Halt!" one of them yelled, firing again. "Halt, or we'll shoot!"

Shoot? Since when are rent-a-cops allowed to shoot? And isn't that halt warning supposed to come just a little ahead of a Dirty Harry–style barrage? Buffy ducked her head down and ran, narrowly staying ahead of the line of bullets that bit into the ground at her heels. She ran in the opposite direction Giles went, heading for the trees.

One of the guys must have been a track star because he ran at her from the side, closing the distance rapidly. "I've got him! I've got him!" His light whipped across Buffy's eyes for just an instant, blinding her. Then he dropped a heavy hand on her shoulder.

Before he could start pulling, Buffy grabbed his thumb and yanked hard. Something popped, but she didn't think she'd broken his thumb. He yelped and let go, but he kept up the chase with the others.

Buffy leaned into her strides, depending on her Slayer abilities and constitution. She began a long loop back to where they'd left Giles's car. *Now if there just aren't any more vampires along the way, and if I don't beat Giles back to the car, we should be good to go.*

Willow looked at the empty bed where Tad had been. *At least, I hope it was Tad. I fed him. I really hope it was Tad.*

The only thing that remained in the bed was the eerie skin that peeled off the creature when the bayberry leaves touched it. Xander played a flashlight over the puddle of goop lying there on the crisp white sheets. He took a pen from his pocket and used it to lift the shedded flesh.

The flesh, or whatever it was, oozed from the end of his pencil and plopped back onto the bedsheet. "Now that's disgusting," he said.

"That," Willow said in a shaky voice, "may have been Baby Tad." Tears wet her eyes.

"Hey," Xander said softly, "don't even be thinking like that."

"I feel so helpless," Willow said, gazing at the empty bed. "I was supposed to be here to take care of him."

"It probably won't make you feel any better, Will," Xander said, "but I don't think most babysitters would have been prepared for this. I mean, this probably isn't covered in the handbook under the old 'Baby Turns into a Winged Monster' section."

"What am I going to do?" Willow asked. She felt herself cratering, no longer able to hold it together.

Xander reached for her and took her into his arms. "We're going to do what we can," he whispered into her ear. "Nothing less. I promise."

Buffy raced out of the forest to Giles's little foreign car. The Watcher sat behind the wheel, examining something he held in his hands.

Still sprinting, her breath coming rapidly, Buffy reached the car and opened the door. She dropped into the passenger seat, gasping. "Drive," she said. "One of those guys back there must be some kind of Olympic hopeful."

"Of course." Giles pocketed whatever it was he held and turned the key. The engine grinded a few times in a spirited effort to start.

Glancing over the back seat, Buffy watched the security guard who'd been on her heels suddenly explode from the dense foliage. He fired two rounds. One of them hit Giles's car in the taillight. "Halt or I'll shoot!" he yelled.

"Decent of him to warn us," Giles said, pumping the accelerator. The engine caught. With the dense forest in front of them, there was no way to drive forward. He had no choice but to go back along the side road past the security guard. He peered through the back window and hesitated. The security guard ran straight for them.

Buffy slammed her foot home on top of Giles's on the accelerator. The little car shivered but the engine performed valiantly, spewing gravel as it sped backward.

"Drive," Buffy said. "He's fast. Trust me."

Giles handled the car easily. A surprised look flitted across the security guard's face, then he threw himself to one side, vanishing into the dense brush as they roared past with a clatter and thump of muffler and shocks.

"Buffy's still not home, but I reached her mom."

Willow glanced up at Xander. "Did you tell her what was going on?"

Xander shook his head. "I didn't see any reason to. There's enough weirdness going on with Buffy's life that I figure her mom doesn't need to know it all."

"Any luck getting ahold of the Campbells?" Cordelia asked, walking into the room with Hutch at her heels.

"No," Willow said, feeling trapped and helpless. Cold dread lined the pit of her stomach like she'd drunk a Slushie way too fast. For a minute she thought she was going to be sick. She glanced at the list of numbers she'd gotten from the Campbells before they'd left. Six numbers of potential places they'd be, including their car phone, and she wasn't able to reach them.

Xander sat beside her on the couch and draped an arm across her shoulders. "They'll turn up."

"We couldn't find any sign of the flying whatever-it-was," Cordelia said.

"But the doors were all locked," Willow said. Noticing the jealous gleam in Cordelia's eyes, she gently pulled away from Xander. "It couldn't have gotten out. It has to be here! We have to find it and make it tell us where Tad is!"

"Will," Xander said softly, "we looked. Cordelia looked, Hutch looked, and I looked." He clenched his fist and returned her gaze full measure. "It's just not here."

The silence that followed that statement hung heavy and still.

A knock sounded on the door and Hutch let two

security guards in. They wore patches that identified them as part of the Wingspread development.

"You the guys who called in the missing baby?" the older guard asked.

"Yeah," Xander said. "Can you help us?"

The man nodded and got a quick description of Tad.

"It's happened again," the younger security guard said, showing fear and disbelief on his face. "Gallivan's going to have our badges for this."

"What's happened again?" Xander asked.

"Nothing," the older guard said, slapping his partner on the shoulder and starting him toward the door. "You guys stay here and let us handle this. If we find anything, you'll know about it."

Xander looked at Willow. "They said *again*."

Willow nodded, not understanding.

Then the phone rang and she thought she was going to jump out of her skin.

CHAPTER 7

"It's been a blast, Giles. We'll have to do it again sometime." Buffy looked at her Watcher more intently when he didn't respond. They'd left the park only a few minutes ago and were now stopped at the curb in front of Buffy's house. "Maybe next time you can bring your attention span. You know, the polite part of you that remembers I'm still breathing?"

Giles's attention seemed consumed by the objects he had in his hands. The silence eventually got through to him even though her words didn't. He looked up at her. "I apologize. I'm probably more distracted than I should be."

"Point." Buffy glanced at the objects he held, recognizing them as the ones he'd found back at the park. "Did you take those from the excavation site?"

Giles looked embarrassed. "Yes, I must admit I did."

"You compromised the integrity of that dig site," Buffy accused, only halfway seriously. "While you were lecturing me about your experiences on the archeological digs you went on, you said the dig sites were supposed to be in violet or ultraviolet or whatever."

"Inviolate. But the circumstances here are extenuating."

Buffy folded her arms. "That sounds like a cop-out."

"Buffy," he said with a trace of annoyance in his voice, "the items I took clearly are not of American-Indian origin. In fact, if I'm correct, they're Russian."

"And that's a big deal?"

Giles made a face. "The Russians were keenly interested in the North American fur trade at one time during the period this country was being settled. So perhaps it's not all that awe-inspiring. But this piece does represent an anomaly. Since the vampires were there as well, my first inclination was to keep this since it didn't fit." Switching on the overhead light, he revealed the object. Black corrosion covered the slim tube. Caps at either end held weirdly shaped characters. "I had to scratch the corrosion off to get at the letters, but they're part of the Cyrillic alphabet. The alphabet of the—"

"Russians," Buffy said. "Got that. How many Russian vampires are hanging out over here?"

"None that I'm aware of. Though that's not to say that an artifact can't have been left here that's worth investigating. This tube is actually silver. You can tell by the black corrosion. It's this color from prolonged exposure to saltwater, and I find that—"

"Giles," Buffy said, stopping his conversation by counting off on her fingers. "Test. Laundry. Spring Blow-Out. The friendship meltdown with Cordelia and Willow. Sleep. I like you and I'm glad you got something that just mystifies the heck out of you, but that's not me. Historical mysteries are really low on my personal interest list."

Giles regretfully slipped the tube into his jacket pocket. "Understood. I'll see you in the morning."

Buffy got out and went up to the porch. Giles waited by the curb till she used her key and let herself into the house. *That's so sweet,* she thought, feeling guilty she'd cut him off short. She should have listened to him a little longer and let him enjoy his moment of glory. *Should've, would've, could've.* She knew Giles understood.

She walked back to the kitchen, thinking about some kind of snack. *Chocolate sounds really good right now. Maybe there's a piece of that cake Mom brought home left.*

The light in the kitchen was on. Intrigued, Buffy dropped her backpack on the sofa and walked into the room. Her mom sat at the kitchen table with a fresh cup of coffee.

"Mom? What are you doing up?" *As if I don't know this has got to be bad.*

"Willow called. There's been some trouble."

* * *

Buffy jogged to the curb in front of the Campbells' home and slowed. Her stomach was all crawly from nervousness and dodging the guards at the main gate. The porch already held a crowd that included Willow, Cordelia, Xander, Oz, and Hutch.

"Thanks for coming, Buffy," Willow said. Her cheeks looked shiny and her eyes looked like she'd been crying.

"Hey," Buffy said softly, "you knew I'd be here. I just wish I could have been here sooner. Mom said you got ahold of the parents." She sat beside her. Willow had been such a source of quiet strength for her during their friendship, she hated to see her so knocked down. "So when are the police going to be here?"

"I don't know," Xander spoke up. "We told the security guards and they said they'd handle things."

"A kidnapping, especially a child's," Oz said on the other side of Willow, "that doesn't just stop with the police. It goes to the FBI too. Pretty much automatically with all the new laws that are out to protect kids. The security guards here were talking about how this wasn't the first kidnapping in the development."

"Not the first?" Buffy was confused and even more scared. "I haven't heard anything about it in the news."

Oz nodded. "Neither has anybody else. Creepy, huh?"

"Somebody's stonewalling somebody," Xander said. "Parents wouldn't keep quiet about their kids getting taken without somebody putting a lot of pressure on them."

Buffy silently agreed, feeling even worse because Willow had gotten caught up in something so bad. *Who would be taking babies, and why? And why wasn't anything being said about it?*

A long black sedan wheeled to a stop in the Campbells' driveway. All the Slayerettes went on alert at once.

A man who looked big enough to play professional football got out from behind the wheel. He wore a dark suit and, despite the lateness of the hour, wraparound dark sunglasses.

Another man got out on the other side. He wore sunglasses and a dark suit as well. They both buttoned their jackets, and from the way the cloth hung, Buffy was willing to bet they carried concealed pistols. *Secret Service? Mafia? Military?* Their moves were crisp and clean.

The driver went back to the rear door and opened it. He scanned the neighborhood while helping a woman and a man out, then stood guard over them as they headed for the door.

"I want my baby, Bryce! I want my baby!" the woman cried and held on to the man beside her. She was a few pounds overweight but still had a good figure and knew how to dress for it. He wore a pinstriped three-piece suit, wire-rimmed glasses, and a receding hairline that branded him as a corporate executive.

He approached Willow, holding on to his wife.

Gray worry lines marked his face. "It's okay, Willow, you can go," he said gently. He handed her an envelope.

Willow, Oz, and Buffy had risen to their feet.

"I can go?" Willow repeated. "Don't you want me to stay around and answer questions from the police?"

"We'll interface with the local authorities," the taller bodyguard said. "There's nothing you can do here. Unless you can name the people who did this."

"A person didn't do this," Willow blurted.

Now that's going to draw some interesting questions, Buffy thought.

Mrs. Campbell suddenly pushed away from her husband, weaving unsteadily toward Willow. "Did you see it?" she demanded. "Did you see the thing that took my baby?"

Before Willow could answer, though, Mr. Campbell pulled his wife back to him. She fought against him briefly, but he whispered something that quieted her.

Mr. Campbell turned to Willow. "The doctor prescribed a mild sedative. It's hitting her harder than we'd anticipated." He led her away.

The bodyguards formed a wall on the porch. "Time to go," the big guy said.

That's a definite cue. Gently, Buffy led Willow away, turning that job over to Oz once he stepped up. "I'll take her home," Oz volunteered. "Make sure she gets something to eat."

Buffy nodded. "Sure." She glanced back at the big house, totally mystified.

Xander dropped into step with Buffy, one arm around Cordelia, who accompanied him. Hutch fell in behind them. "Let me see if I've got this straight. Willow gets hired to baby-sit baby. Watches baby. Watches baby turn into some kind of monster thing. It disappears. Mom and Dad come home *way* later than you'd think caring parents should after they're told about the abduction of their son. They also have Mutt and Jeff, two really mean looking guys who're zealous about guarding the Campbells. They don't call the police. They don't call the FBI. That about sum it up?"

"Yes."

"I can sum it up for you in one word," Cordelia said. "Weirdness." She smiled. "But, lucky for us, this isn't our problem anymore."

Buffy nodded reluctantly, her thoughts whirling. She knew she couldn't just let go of the thing now. Even if she was able, Willow wouldn't. It only took one glance at her friend to know that.

Cordelia looked meaningfully at Buffy. "Translation: this isn't your problem either. Moving on to more cheery news, have you decided what you're going to wear to the party Friday night?"

Willow shot Cordelia a look of disbelief, but being Willow, she didn't actually give vent to any of her shock.

Let it go, Buffy told herself. *This is Cordelia. She lives in her own world.* "Actually," she said, "I've been meaning to talk to you about that." *Maybe it wouldn't hurt to burst her bubble. Just a little.*

"Tell me you're not going to throw in with the tree-huggers," Cordelia said. "Green is *not* a color someone with your coloring would want to spend any real time with."

"Look," Buffy said. "There's another problem. Vampires are gathering around Weatherly Park, and they're looking for something. If we try to have the party there while that's going on, the only party favors we'll be passing out will be body bags."

Baby Tad smiled up at Willow, kicking his tiny boots as she rubbed lotion onto his skin. The clean smell of the baby, so fresh, made her smile back. He felt soft and vulnerable in her hands.

She lifted him up when she had him dressed again, talking to him in that singsong voice she'd learned all babies liked. He gurgled at her, laughing so hard his eyes watered.

Then, without warning, he reached a small fist up and tore one of his little chubby cheeks off, revealing the creature within.

"Willow," *the creature promised,* "we're not done with you."

Willow screamed—

And woke up in the darkness of her own bedroom. She felt her heart hammering inside her chest, and was cold despite the blankets covering her.

Slowly, afraid something was going to jump out at her, she craned her head around to scan the room.

The clock/radio by the bed said it was 2:17 A.M. She closed her eyes and tried to go back to sleep. She knew it wasn't going to happen. Bone-tired, she staggered from her bed and into the hallway. She went to the bathroom by memory, wanting a glass of water for her dry throat.

Her heart still hammered when she turned on the light and filled one of the disposable cups hanging on the wall. As she drank, she glanced at the mirror above the sink.

Baby Tad stood in there, something he wasn't able to do in real life. *It's scrying. It's a witch thing ... only without the surface of water that's usually needed to scry.* Willow forced herself to keep from totally freaking and tried to study the scene revealing itself to her.

Fog shrouded the area where Baby Tad was, but she got the distinct impression there were a lot of plants around him. He stuck all the fingers on his right hand into his mouth and sucked on them. He waved, then turned around and walked away, disappearing into the fog and shrubbery.

Breaking free of the trance that held her while she looked into the mirror, Willow retreated to her room, turned on the light, and did the only thing she knew to do when things turned totally weird and scary. She called Buffy.

Buffy walked through the hallways of Sunnydale High like a zombie the next morning. It was after first period and she still wasn't awake. She'd talked to Willow for nearly three hours last night—*make that this morning*—trying to keep her friend calm.

Smothering a yawn, the Slayer walked into the school library, crossed the room, and sat on one of the chairs across from the main desk. She held her books tightly, trying to offset the chill that threatened to claim her.

"You look terrible," Giles said.

"Thanks," Buffy replied. She noticed the dark circles under Giles's eyes and grew concerned. Despite the physical dangers she faced on a regular basis, she knew the Watcher frequently pushed himself to the limit as well. "Didn't you get any sleep last night?"

"Very little. The studies I entered into turned out to be quite demanding. But those hours last night appear to have been time well invested, if not entirely rewarding."

"You found out why the vamps are so interested in the park?" Buffy's spirits rose.

"No. But I did find out the tube I discovered there is definitely Russian." Giles reached back into the office and opened his desk drawer. He took a baggie containing the silver cylinder out and laid it on the desk. "It's quite interesting."

"Meaning it has nothing at all to do with vampires."

The Watcher gave her a wry smile. "Unfortunately, no. But it does prey on the imagination."

"Not the imagination of this one. We've also got another bit of weirdness going on." Quickly, Buffy outlined the events that had happened at the Campbell house. Captivated by the story, Giles left the silver cylinder on the desk. As Buffy was finishing the story, Willow and Oz joined them.

"The parents requested you *not* go to the proper authorities?" Giles asked when she finished. "That's not right. They could be exposing the child to even more danger." He turned his attention to Willow. "Can you describe the creature?"

Willow did, in great detail, accompanied by shuddering that prompted Oz to drop his arm over her shoulders.

"You're sure you've never seen anything like it?" Giles asked. "You've seen nearly as many of the books I keep here as I have."

Willow shook her head. "Trust me, I'd know if I saw that thing before. And I'll know if I see it again."

"Let's plan on *not* seeing it again," Oz told her.

"You said it knew you?" Giles persisted.

"It called me by name. It told me that what I was doing for the park was good, but it wasn't enough."

"The park?" Giles repeated, glancing at Buffy. "You didn't tell me about this."

"That's because I wasn't told," Buffy responded. During her association with the Watcher, she'd gotten good at delivering details even when she'd only gotten a brief glimpse of something.

"I guess I kind of forgot it in all the confusion," Willow admitted. "Actually . . . it said what I was doing for the *forest*, not the park."

"Buffy told me it changed shape."

Willow nodded. "When I dropped the bayberry leaves on it. Bayberry is a herb that witches use to—"

"To free someone from the power of another," Giles said. "I know. Maybe the cylinder I found last night does tie into this. Tell me, are you familiar with the legend of the Changeling?"

CHAPTER 8

"**T**hat's one of the most prevalent myths about faeries," Willow said, locking her eyes with the Watcher's. "Do you think Tad was a Changeling?"

Faeries? Changeling? "Hold it," Buffy said. "Time out. Reality check." She glanced from Giles to Willow. "I'm lost. Vampires, I know. Same with zombies, mummies, and a host of other mondo uglies, but this whole Changeling thing throws me. Is it like the time that Xander joined the hyena pack?"

"No," Giles answered. "That was demonic possession, not changelings. There's a big difference. What do you know about faeries?"

"They're little guys," Buffy said, thinking back to her childhood when such things had fascinated her. "Wings. They hide a lot, play tricks on you. Maybe wear green most of the time?" *Not sure about that one.* "Have a thing for shoes and teeth?" *Those,* she felt, *were dead-solid locks.*

Giles sighed. "Didn't you read faery tales when you were growing up?"

"We had alternate entertainment that didn't involve reading. *Smurfs, Scooby-Doo, Duck Tales*—"

"Enough. Trust me when I say there are dozens of different faeries that have been written about during centuries of literature."

"This is going to be the every-child-should-be-issued-a-library-card riff, isn't it?" Buffy asked.

"I'll forgo that simple pleasure. In all of the narratives concerning faeries, we are shown there are basically two kinds of faeries."

"Good ones and bad ones," Buffy said, perking up. "See? I'm a quick study."

"That's because when it comes to slaying," Xander said as he joined them, "that's about all there is of anything. What are we talking about?"

"Giles thinks I saw a faery last night," Willow said.

"Will, you're taking entirely too much comfort in that answer," Buffy said. Or maybe she was just entirely too *uncomfortable* with it.

Willow turned on her. "You drive stakes through the hearts of vampires on a daily—make that, nightly—basis, and you're trying to talk me out of believing in faeries? Don't go Scully on me, Buffy."

"You're right," Buffy said, acknowledging her lack

of open-mindedness. "I just don't want things to get any more out of hand than they already are."

"They can't," Willow said quietly. "Tad is missing."

Buffy nodded, understanding. *Oh Willow, I just wish you realized this can't be your fault.*

"Hey," Xander said in the silence that followed, "I always liked the story about the cobbler and the elves."

"Elves," Giles said, seizing the opportunity to steer the conversation again. "They're considered by some experts to be another incarnation of faeries. Along with pixies and brownies. Myths and legends have been around about the little people ever since people started exchanging stories. Beginning with pre-Christian cultures researchers believe faeries were made up to explain acts and forces in nature. The Celts were among those who postulated faeries were actually spirits of the dead, drawn from their graves. In Iceland, Norse mythology had it that maggots turned into Light and Dark elves."

"Good and evil," Buffy said, getting attention back to the fact that she knew her stuff.

"Exactly. As you know from your own existence, Buffy, there are forces at work that constantly align champions of the Light and Dark. Though, that is not to say that those champions are incorruptible or that those of the dark are without salvation. Post-Christian mythology suggests that faeries were created when Eve was washing her children and God came calling. Not wanting the dirty children revealed, she hid them in the forest. When she was asked if all the children were present, she replied in the affirmative. Then God punished her for lying and for hiding the children, telling her that the ones that she'd hidden would forever remain hidden from the eyes of men."

"Now there's a story to tell your kids when it comes bath time," Xander said. "It beats all that stuff you hear about potatoes growing in your ears."

Buffy pointed to a nearby chair. "Sit."

Xander sat.

"There are other stories," Willow went on, "that suggested faeries were unbaptized children, fallen angels, or druids who refused to convert from their pagan beliefs."

"Exactly," Giles agreed. "Science even got into the act with their own explanation, suggesting that when the Celts invaded some of the lands in northern Europe they fought against a race of much smaller people."

"Picts?" Oz asked. "They were small and around at about the same time."

"Quite possibly." Giles brightened at the idea someone other than Willow knew this territory. "At any rate, the speculative historians suggest that the legends not only of faeries but also of giants came from those encounters. Traditionally, iron weapons harm faeries. At that time, the Celts had iron weapons while the smaller race didn't."

"Interesting," Buffy said in a way that suggested it

was not. "How does all of this help us with Will?"

"Wings," Willow said. "Most faeries have wings. That thing last night had wings. It also hit me with some kind of dust. I remember it reaching into a little leather pouch it had and flinging it into my face."

"That's another really common theme concerning faeries," Giles said. "Faery dust that makes mortals sleep. But the biggest connection we seem to have here is the myth of the Changeling."

"That's where they traded a faery baby for a human baby, right?" Oz asked.

"Yes," Giles answered, clearly pleased. "One of the best and greatest tricks of the faeries was to replace faery children for human children. These changelings, if you will, looked exactly like the children they replaced. Except that they were supposed to have huge appetites, malicious natures, and some kind of deformity. Did you notice any deformities on the child you baby-sat last night?"

Willow shook her head. "No. He was just the perfect baby. He smelled clean and felt soft. He was really no trouble at all." Her voice broke. "I'm sorry. It's just that—just that—"

"We know, Will," Buffy sympathized.

"There's more to it," Willow said to Giles. "Buffy already knows because I called her last night. I had a vision—"

"Or maybe a dream," Buffy put in.

"Or maybe a dream," Willow agreed. "But it didn't feel like a dream."

"Tell me what you think you saw," Giles encouraged.

Willow explained about Tad and the plants. "I think it was a vision," she said. "I haven't really experimented with scrying, but I know what it is."

"I don't," Xander said.

"Scrying," Willow said, "is an art attributed to witches. By looking into a bowl of water, a crystal ball, or any kind of reflective surface, a trained witch can see other places or other times. The past and the future."

"But you're not a trained witch," Xander pointed out.

"She's got skills," Oz said. "We've all seen that."

It's true, Buffy realized. *They've saved our lives more than once. We don't know what Willow's full capabilities will be.*

"Assuming that it was a vision," Giles said, "you must ask yourself why you observed it. You weren't actively pursuing such a thing."

Willow shook her head.

"Okay, let's leave that there for the moment, shall we?" Giles leaned forward and picked the silver cylinder from the desk. "Buffy and I know from observation last night that several of the vampires in the area are actively seeking *something* in or around Weatherly Park. During our excursion last night, chance provided me with this." He spilled the corroded silver cylinder from the baggie onto the table.

"You took that from the excavation site?" Xander asked.

"It didn't belong," Giles replied, slightly defensive.

"Bet the people responsible for getting all that stuff out of the ground don't feel that way about it." Xander grinned smugly, giving his who's-in-hot-water-this-time look.

"As it turns out, the information contained within this cylinder may come in handy now." Giles carefully pried one end of the cylinder off, revealing the hollow recess inside. He tapped it a couple times, then tightly rolled sheets of some kind of writing paper came out.

"What is that?" Buffy leaned forward.

"A journal," the Watcher replied, "written on vellum. Cured sheepskin, to be exact." He carefully placed the sheets on the desk and held them spread out with one hand. "Nearly all of it is in Russian. You can recognize the Cyrillic alphabet quite easily."

"Of course," Buffy deadpanned. "Do you read Russian?"

"Not enough to get through all of this," Giles admitted. "But I picked up enough to allow me to get the gist of what's contained on these sheets. I've contacted people who might be able to do a complete translation. I'll know more this evening."

"So give it up," Xander said.

"Primarily these deal with warnings. However, I was able to decipher a bit more. It warns of an unearthly terror."

Yadda yadda yadda, Buffy thought.

"Did you get a name to go with that?" Oz asked.

"No. I'm hoping the people I've contacted will be able to help with that. I'm certain whatever it is will be named in this text. But there is another word I was able to recognize. *Domovoi.*"

"What's that?" Buffy asked.

Giles sipped his tea. "It's a Russian faery."

Xander shifted in his chair uneasily. "Heads up, people, we're about to be approached by the Gestapo."

Buffy turned toward the door and watched as Principal Snyder entered the library. *An unexpected visit of this sort we don't need.*

"Mr. Giles," Snyder said unctuously, "and some of my more favored students." He offered a smile totally devoid of sincerity. "I don't know if you've heard the stories yet, but it appears there was something of a hoo-raw that took place in Weatherly Park last night."

"When?" Buffy asked before she could stop herself. *Was it the security guards we saw last night?* She hoped it wasn't her fault.

"Miss Summers, I didn't know you had such an interest in current events. To answer your question, I'm told that a few of *our* students engaged in vandalism at the excavation site near Weatherly Park some time after midnight."

It wasn't us. Buffy breathed a silent sigh of relief.

"As a result," Snyder went on, "Mr. Gallivan is doubling the security."

Great, Buffy thought sourly, *more vampire kibble.*

"Also," Snyder continued, "the school is no longer in a position to sanction in any way the Spring Blow-Out that so many of you may be looking forward to." He smiled broadly. "You have my condolences. I'll be making the announcement public in the next few minutes."

"How do they know it was someone from this school?" Xander asked.

"Mr. Harris," Snyder said, "Gallivan Industries security guards caught the students responsible for sabotaging the bulldozers, *and* they identified them. There's no question about what school they're from." He switched his gaze to Willow. "I believe they were associates of yours, Miss Rosenberg. Possibly some of the same people you staged your Protest in the Park and for the Park with last week. And if I find out you had anything to do with organizing that attack against Gallivan Industries, I'll see that you're charged as well."

When Snyder turned smartly on his heel and left the library, Buffy let out a breath. *Well, at least there's no reason to worry about the vampires getting more students.*

Xander looked at Willow. "'Just a peaceful demonstration,' you said. 'Somebody has to try to preserve the park,' you said."

Willow opened her mouth to reply, but Oz interrupted.

"Hey, we'll deal later. Save the park, don't save the park—that's not really going to matter if we're getting involved in a vampire/faery turf war over that forest. Right?"

"He does have a point," Buffy said. *Why couldn't things come like one problem at a time?*

"Turf war?" Xander echoed. "You make it sound like something out of a Coppola film. *The Faery Godfather.* 'Let me kiss your ring, Faery Godfather.'" He was getting into it.

"Perhaps," Giles said, "we could talk about what we do know."

"What are domovoi?" Buffy asked. "You said they were some kind of Russian faery."

"They were considered helpful faeries in the Russian households who believed," the Watcher said. "They watched over and guarded the household. Usually they lived behind the stove, though sometimes they lived under doorsteps. A domovoi's wife was reputed to live in the cellar."

"There's equality for you," Xander said.

"Primarily, they were thought to be active at night," Giles continued, ignoring Xander's comment. "Supposedly, the hairier the domovoi was, the more luck it was purported to bring. And if the family moved to a new home, the family was supposed to take brands from the old stove to light the stove in the new house."

"To bring the domovoi to the new house?" Oz asked.

"Exactly."

"And what does this have to do with the baby disappearances?" Willow asked.

Giles shook his head. "I haven't the slightest idea. But we can't overlook the juxtaposition of events and the significance of the vampires searching the area. Things that look related often are, even though you'd think in all probability that they aren't."

"So where do we go from here?" Xander piped up. "It looks like my Friday night is going to be free."

"We now have a couple avenues open to us," Giles suggested. "I shall endeavor to discover what I can about this mysterious note and whatever information it might contain. Perhaps, Willow, you and Buffy could see what you can ferret out on other kidnapped children of Gallivan Industries employees. The cryptic comment you overheard from the security guards points us in that direction. Though I don't recall anything mentioned in the local media."

"Gallivan might have hushed it up," Oz said. "From the way those guys were talking, it sounded like they're taking orders from him. After all, we haven't heard anything about Tad and we've been listening to the news."

"If that's the case and Gallivan has had a hand in things," Giles said, "it may be hard to learn anything."

"Gallivan hiding the fact that babies are disappearing." Xander smiled, his dark eyes flashing. "Man, you gotta love a conspiracy."

"Yes, well," Giles said, "you have to remember that if there is some kind of conspiracy afoot here, they'll have people in place whose job it is to ensure whatever information they're hiding isn't found out. Be cautious."

The possibility troubled Buffy a lot. "But if they're hiding the fact that someone's taking children of Gallivan Industries employees, why keep it quiet?" She didn't like thinking how much danger the babies might be in.

"That is the question, isn't it?" Giles agreed.

No one had any answers.

CHAPTER 9

"**A**voiding mystery meat day in the school cafeteria?"

Buffy glanced up as Xander joined her and Willow at one of the tables in the student break area.

"Sort of," Buffy agreed. Actually, she'd hoped to have some time alone with Willow. Her best bud was taking the loss of Baby Tad really hard.

"Potluck," Willow said. "Everybody was supposed to bring something." She indicated the chicken-spread sandwiches she'd made and the bowl of fruit and vegetables Buffy had cut up.

"Hey," Xander said, dropping into a chair, "I kind of figured that. So I came prepared." He took a Snickers bar and a package of Corn Nuts from his pocket. "I think we have enough to go around."

"Corn Nuts?" Buffy asked.

Xander shrugged. "I considered Skittles for the

fruit group, but I decided to go with the Corn Nuts so it'd be more balanced."

"More balanced?" Willow echoed. "How can those things possibly resemble a balanced meal?"

Xander held up the Snickers bar. "Here you've got peanuts, also known as protein. Chewy caramel nougat, also known as dairy. And something in there must be close to the bread group. The Corn Nuts are vegetables."

"Let me see that package," Buffy said skeptically.

Xander pushed the Corn Nuts across.

Buffy examined the package. "The closest these things ever came to a vegetable was the oil they were fried in."

"The name says *corn*," Xander argued. "Who knew? I'm telling you, there should be truth in advertising. Get back to basics, that kind of thing." He glanced at the sandwiches and fruit. "So okay, I've anted up. Am I in or out?"

Willow handed him half a sandwich. "In."

Buffy pulled the top off the fruit and vegetable container and offered it. "In."

"Great," Xander replied, tearing open the Corn Nuts package. "Who wants the first handful?"

"I don't think so," Buffy said. "How's Cordelia taking the announcement about the Spring Blow-Out?"

"You know how the talk-show guests on the 'I'm Cheating on You with Your Best Friend' episodes react when they're told?"

"Yeah," Willow said quietly.

"Not even that good," Xander assured her.

Buffy glanced back at the hallway and watched as students pulled one of the Spring Blow-Out banners hanging around the school from the wall. Principal Snyder was watching nearby, a satisfied smile on his face. "At least somebody's happy."

"Oh, I don't think Cordelia's *totally* put out," Xander said. "Banning the Spring Blow-Out seems to have made it more popular than ever. She's even got a band lined up."

"I thought she wanted Oz and his band." Dingoes Ate My Baby played semi-regularly at the Bronze.

"She thought there might be some conflict of interest on Oz's part. . . ." Xander glanced at Willow.

"That's ridiculous," Willow said. "I don't have anything against the Spring Blow-Out. It's Gallivan's intentions to turn the park into Amusement City that I'm against."

"Don't tell me," Xander protested. "Tell Cordy."

"Closely related to the advice to chew off your own foot when you're caught in a trap," Buffy said.

"I'd rather face the trap," Willow admitted. "And the chewing." She picked at her sandwich.

Buffy glanced at her friend and felt bad. *So much is going wrong for her right now*. She thought about it a moment. *Like tracking down all the vampires gathering in the park will be a picnic*.

"Cordelia's going to be even less cheery when we do another protest at the park today," Willow said. "We're supposed to get media coverage after what happened last night."

"Did you hear who was caught?" Buffy asked.

"Lance Torrance and Kelly Carruthers," Willow said.

"The pair voted most likely to join subversive activities involving munitions?" Xander asked.

"I don't think they've been at a single rally," Willow said. "But they told police they were with the protest last week."

"It gave them a reason to do what they did," Buffy said, understanding.

"An excuse to blow something up, you mean," Xander put in. "Remember what they did to the chemistry lab last year? If it wasn't for all the other weirdness that goes on around here, they'd have been expelled for life."

"Buffy, I'm kind of thinking about going to see the Campbells today," Willow said. "To see if there was any news. Or anything I can do. I was hoping you could go with me."

"I'm there." Buffy didn't want her facing the parents on her own.

"It's still going on."

Buffy and Willow stepped down the street from the security gates blocking the entrance into the Wingspread edition. School had ended, eventually, with more of a whimper than a bang and the two friends had set out for the Campbells'. "What?"

"The visions of Baby Tad," Willow said in a soft voice. "I've seen a half-dozen of them today. In windows. The bathroom mirror. Stainless steel surfaces in lab. Even once in the flame of a Bunsen burner."

"Maybe it's just memory."

Willow shook her head. "Not memory. Memory feels different. Like listening to a favorite song you haven't heard in a while. This is more like listening to a recent remake of an eighties pop tune. It's the same thing, just really different."

"What do you think it is?"

Buffy noticed the line of cars at the gate. The security guard was checking them through cautiously. "I don't know. Maybe I'm kind of tied to the baby. Because of the guilt I feel. What scares me is that I have to wonder if these visions are put there by the faeries."

"Because you're the one who's supposed to help them get to Home base?"

"Home*stone,*" Willow said.

"That could be it. Couldn't it?"

"Maybe."

Buffy looked at Willow, seeing the gray fatigue clinging to her features. "Maybe. But don't worry. We're going to get to the bottom of whatever it is."

"I just can't stop thinking about Tad," Willow said. "I keep thinking about how scared he must be. Wondering if they're taking care of him, feeding him. Or if he's alone somewhere or even . . . alive."

"That's a lot to think about, so try to think about it positively. Just remember that he's out there somewhere, and that we're doing our best to get him back where he belongs. We may even get some answers here. Especially if we can get Mrs. Campbell alone. She seemed like she was ready to talk to someone last night."

Willow walked ahead, stopping beside the security guard.

"Hi," he said from behind mirror-lensed sunglasses. "I need you to tell me who you're here to see."

"Mr. and Mrs. Bryce Campbell." Willow fumbled nervously in her purse for her ID. "I've got a driver's license here."

"That won't be necessary," the security guard said. "I'm afraid I'm going to have to ask you to leave."

"Why?" Buffy asked. "Is there some kind of problem?"

"No problem," the security guard said. "It's just that the Campbells no longer live here."

"They *moved?*" Willow asked.

"Earlier today," the security guard said. "I saw the moving truck take out the last of their things when I got here this morning."

"Do you know where they went?" Buffy asked. *Why would they leave? Where would they go? Had they got the baby back and not told anyone?*

"No. But that would be privileged information even if I did."

"Do you know why they moved?"

"No," the guard said. "Gallivan Industries moved them out. That's all I know."

"Gallivan Industries?"

"Right. I guess it must be some kind of corporate thing. This is the fourth family that Gallivan has moved out since the first of the month."

Buffy looked at Willow. "Road trip to the school library?"

"I'm there."

"The first of the month was when Gallivan Industries announced their plans for the Weatherly Park area."

Buffy sat behind Willow in the school library and watched as her friend brought up screen after screen of papers and news articles. They'd been there little less than an hour and Willow's research skills resulted in a lot of information about Gallivan Industries. It was strange that Giles wasn't there, but he had his own mysteries he was pursuing.

"So we can assume the first of the kidnappings took place just after that," Buffy said.

"We can make that assumption because we want to," Willow cautioned, "but there's nothing concrete that says that."

None of the papers they'd searched through so far mentioned *any* kidnappings, even ones that weren't related to Gallivan Industries.

"Gallivan Industries came into Sunnydale almost a year ago," Willow said, looking at her notes. "The parent company is out of Houston, Texas. They specialize in property management and commercial development."

Quiet filled the cavernous library, broken only by the hum of the computer in front of Buffy and Willow. "Do they handle private residences?" Buffy asked.

Willow shook her head. "Business pages are such dry reading. I've been through most of them, but I haven't found anything like that yet. I e-mailed all the files to my home computer. I'll take another look tonight."

"Somebody sold Gallivan Industries employees homes in Wingspread," Buffy said. "I'll do the phone thing tonight. Pretend I'm a new Gallivan Industries employee coming into the area on a house-buying spree."

"That means you're going to miss the protest at Weatherly Park today."

Whoops! "Can't do both, Willow. Most of the real estate agents' offices close by five or six. Which would you rather I do?"

"Call the real estate agents," Willow agreed. "Save the park, save the children. There's no choice there. Let me know if you find out anything."

Buffy paced the kitchen in her home while she made the calls after Willow went on to Weatherly Park. The first call she made was to the management office at the Wingspread. Presenting herself as a potential buyer, she asked what real estate agents handled sales in the community. Luckily, there were only four.

The second real estate agent she called, Pierce Properties, turned out to be the one she wanted.

"Yes, we've closed deals on eight properties in the Wingspread during the past year for other Gallivan Industries employees," the cheery woman at the other end of the phone assured her. "All of them have been very happy with their purchases."

Buffy continued pacing, noticing how easy it was

playing private eye when the person giving information was trying desperately to make a sale. "My . . . husband's really new to the corporation, so we don't really know anyone. And he's so busy with his new job and all those . . . responsibilities that he can't take the time to introduce me around." *That sounded believable, didn't it? Now to pour on the motivation.* "He got such a big salary that he's nervous not to be there for them anytime they call. You know how that is."

"Gallivan Industries appears to be very generous," the real estate agent agreed.

"He told me to go pick a house," Buffy said, playing out the dumb blonde role she'd chosen. "I mean, it's that kind of money: just go pick a house. And he told me that some of the employees were buying houses in the Wingspread."

"You couldn't do much better than the Wingspread," the agent said. "It's a gated community. Very strict. And there's a twenty-four-hour security network."

"Do they have much trouble out there?"

"None that I've heard of."

"Good, because we've got two kids," Buffy said. *Two? Wouldn't one have been enough?* She didn't know where that had come from.

"Really?" the woman said. "And what are the names of the little darlings?"

Almost caught off-guard, Buffy searched the counters for help. "Ginger," she said, that from the spice rack, "and little Joy," that from the dishwashing detergent.

"You sound very proud of them."

"I am. They're always just kind of . . . right there, you know."

"I can show you some places in the Wingspread," the agent offered.

"That'd be great, but before you do, I'd like to talk to some of the other women who've bought houses out there. Just to get a feel for things. Do you have a list of satisfied clients or something?" As she talked, Buffy got the feeling that all she needed to do to complete the role was twirl her hair in her fingers.

"Yes we do. And we've also got permission to give their names out. It's part of the agreement the Wingspread has with its new arrivals and the real estate companies. We'll need your permission when you buy in to the neighborhood too."

"That won't be any problem," Buffy said. "Could I have the names?"

The agent gave them, including phone numbers.

"I say Lance and Kelly had the right idea! We ought to nuke Gallivan and his work crews before they can get started! This was our park a long time before they decided to come in and tear it down!"

Willow hurried through the group of kids gathered in front of the merry-go-round she'd chosen to use as their center stage in Weatherly Park. Full dark had started to descend over the area and some of the students were using flashlights. Others had brought electric lanterns. Most of them were gathered at the speaker's platform. "Excuse me. Pardon me. Sorry."

Luckily, the speech only found a few supporters in

the crowd. Willow joined Craig Jefferies on the merry-go-round, struggling to keep her balance as it twisted.

Craig was one of the big guys on campus, a football player and sometime jerk. Willow couldn't remember him ever coming to one of the previous gatherings against the sale of the park. He was tall and broad, with short-clipped blond hair dyed sapphire blue on the ends. He wore a gray ROTC tee and camouflage pants.

"You know what you need?" Craig asked her. "A PA system. One that'll knock the socks off everybody out here."

"Uh, no," Willow said. "That would be wrong." *So wrong!* She lowered her voice even more, knowing she was risking a scene. "And Craig, what I'd like to do here is . . . present a positive atmosphere where people can do something . . . good." *There, that wasn't a concept that was too difficult to grasp, was it?* "I don't want to get them psyched up for an assault on Frankenstein's castle."

Craig grinned and pointed out at the local television station van only now pulling up to a stop at the side of the park. "A little torch waving, a few pitchforks, you'd have a major following in no time, Rosenberg. People would believe in you."

"I don't want them to believe in me," Willow corrected. "I want them to believe in the park."

"People believe in individuals, not movements. The way soldiers believe in commanding officers," Craig said.

"Hey, Craig," Oz said, springing up onto the merry-go-round. "Sounds like you've been listening to the recruitment guys or you've seen *Small Soldiers* one too many times."

"A movement like this, taking on corrupt corporations, doesn't need any sissy-boys in it," Craig challenged.

"Excuse me," Willow said, "but this was kind of a save-the-park thing, not some call to battle."

"It went beyond that," Craig said, "when two of our warriors fell to the enemy last night."

"Media," Oz whispered to Willow.

Willow glanced toward the street and saw the news channel getting out of the van. She recognized G. T. Rockett, one of the roving reporters often featured on the program, by his permed dark hair, goatee, and dazzling smile. He wore a dark blue suit and gave directions to the camcorder and sound crew following him.

"You hold on to that thought," Willow said to Craig, "and I'll get back to you."

Oz led her through the crowd.

"Why do I always get the image of Craig looking like a commando?" she asked. "One of those special-forces types with a knife in his teeth?"

Oz shook his head. "This is Craig, remember? It wouldn't be a knife. It'd be a stick of dynamite."

Willow could imagine that. "But it would be lit."

Oz smiled encouragement at her. "On both ends."

"Don't go soft on these people, Rosenberg," the football player called after her in a harsh voice.

"They can't come in here and run roughshod over citizens willing to stand up for their rights. Not if we can present a unified front."

A few more supportive yells and whistles came from the crowd, but Willow hoped that was because so many of them spotted the arrival of the news personnel. The situation suddenly had the potential of a total negative and she really didn't know what she was going to do about that. *If anything* could *be done.*

Willow stepped off the merry-go-round toward G. T. Rockett. The reporter turned toward her as the girl he was talking to pointed Willow out.

A wave of booing started in the crowd, growing in intensity. Looking around the reporter, Willow saw Hector Gallivan step out of a limousine parked behind the news van. He looked tall and imposing in the glare of the light coming from inside the luxury car.

Definitely not good, she thought.

CHAPTER 10

"Hey, Mom," Buffy said while raiding the refrigerator. She spotted an apple down in the crisper that looked good, if not overly appetizing, and claimed it. "I'm probably going to be out really late tonight. So don't wait up, okay?"

"You didn't say anything about plans tonight." Her mother sat at the dining table with portfolios spread around her.

"Not really plans." Buffy looked at her mom and gestured to the black windsuit she wore. Her backpack sat at her feet. A couple newly sharpened stakes stuck out the top.

Her mom didn't look happy about the situation. "Is someone going with you?"

"Yeah." *Demons, vampires, that sort of crowd . . .*

"Be careful."

"I'll be home soon as I can." Buffy turned and left,

not wanting to drag out the good-bye any longer than it had to be. Both of them knew that each time she stepped out the door to go slaying could be the last time they saw each other, but they couldn't act that way. The emotional fallout would have been too much. *I think I'd really love settling for the traditional problems between a mother and her daughter. Dress lengths, guys, behavior, guys, grades . . .*

She felt a gust of cold wind at her back. She turned, her hands coming up automatically.

"Going somewhere?" Angel stood in the deep shadows staining the front yard. He wore a lightweight duster over his usual dark wardrobe.

Buffy shrugged. "Got to do an errand kind of thing." Every time she was around him it was electric.

"Anything to do with what's going on at Weatherly Park?"

"Maybe. What do you know about Weatherly Park?"

"Not much. I've heard a few people talking. I'm not in with the usual suspects in something like this."

Buffy knew that. Angel's particular path had turned away from the normal pursuits of Sunnydale's vampire crowd. "So what have you heard?"

"That you staked a dozen vampires last night. You and some other guy I figure had to be Giles." He shrugged. "I thought I'd come around and see how you were doing. You're up against some really terrible odds."

"That's the par on this gig," Buffy said. "Just one to a generation, remember? The loneliest number."

"Not tonight," Angel told her. "Tonight, I'll cover your back."

That thought made Buffy feel better than she wanted to. *To have and yet not to have. . . . It was terrible.* "The first part of this is going to be boring—"

"Not with the company."

Buffy smiled at the compliment, yet at the same time it hurt her. They could never have again what they'd once had.

"Deal," she said, setting out at a brisk pace. "I'll fill you in as we go."

Willow watched Hector Gallivan step through the crowd. The student body for the most part backed off immediately, and the four bodyguards flanking him guaranteed no one would get close enough to touch him.

He too wore a dark suit. His hair was combed straight back, black on top and steel gray on the sides. The square-cut jaw was his most prominent feature.

"Hello, G.T." Gallivan stuck out a hand and took the reporter's.

"Hello, Mr. Gallivan," Rockett said. "This is an unexpected surprise."

"A lot of things have been unexpected lately," the industrialist said. He turned his attention to Willow.

She felt like melting, feeling the electricity in the

man's gaze. Before she knew it, Oz stepped up beside her and slid his hand in hers, unseen by anyone else. Just having him there made her feel confident.

The other students crowded up, swiftly forming a circle with their flashlights and lanterns. The bodyguards, all big men with military-style haircuts, surrounded Willow, Oz, Rockett, and Gallivan, creating an island in the middle of all the people.

Rockett gestured frantically to his camcorder operator. "We had no idea you were going to be here this evening," the reporter said. "This way we can present a more balanced piece."

"Actually," Gallivan said, not breaking eye contact with Willow. "I'm not here to debate the issues at hand in a public forum."

That surprised Willow because she'd thought he'd put in an appearance to steal the show. *Of course, he's already done that to an extent just by showing up,* she realized. The idea that he was manipulating *her* show put more resolve in her and she stood straighter.

"Maybe you'd like to tell us what you are here for," Rockett said.

Almost casually, one of the bodyguards seemed to inadvertently step between Gallivan and Rockett. The reporter backed away reluctantly.

"No," Gallivan said. "I'm not here for public comment." He nodded at Willow. "It's Miss Rosenberg, I'm told."

Willow nodded. She'd never heard anyone say her name like that.

"If you have a few moments, I'd like to talk to you." Gallivan gazed at her with dark eyes. "Maybe you could join me in my car."

"No," Oz answered quickly.

Gallivan looked at him, then back at Willow.

"I don't think so," Willow said. *That sounded better than a flat no, didn't it? Gallivan's not a guy used to no,* she told herself. But there was no way she was going anywhere with him by herself.

Gallivan lowered his voice. "Not even if we talk about what you saw at the Campbell house?"

Buffy rang the doorbell and waited on the porch with Angel. The house looked like all the others in the Wingspread edition except for the patches of dying yellow grass and the dead plants in the flower-beds.

Angel stood at Buffy's side. On the way over she'd told him the stories of the park and the creature Willow had encountered. He hadn't had any answers, but Buffy just liked the way they fell into the old routine of talking.

Just as Buffy was about to ring the doorbell again, the door opened. The woman who answered it was dressed in a robe and slippers. *She looks terminally ill,* Buffy thought, trying to hide her shock.

"You're the woman who called me? About buying in to the development?"

Buffy nodded. "If this is a bad time maybe we could come back—"

"No," the woman said in a worn voice. She was in her late twenties, but looked ten years older. "It's just that there aren't any good times." She waved them in.

Buffy followed, but Angel had trouble at the door. As a vampire, he had to be invited into someone's house. He stood on the porch helplessly, waiting. Buffy hesitated, not knowing what to do.

"Aren't you coming?" the woman asked.

Buffy saw the resistance fall away from Angel. He stepped inside. "He's kind of shy sometimes," Buffy said, reaching for his hand.

"That's unusual," the woman said. "Hector Gallivan generally hires people who're self-starters. I'm Maggie Chapin." She led them into a living room that was littered with boxes and clothing. She cleared off a section of the sofa and gestured them to it.

"You haven't finished moving in?" Buffy asked. "The real estate agent said you'd bought your house a few months ago."

"We did." Maggie sat in an old-fashioned rocker and drew her feet up under her. "Now Philip is moving out. I'm staying until the judge orders me out. Maybe even till the sheriff comes and makes me move."

"I'm sorry," Buffy said. She glanced around the house, seeing how much in disarray everything was despite the luxurious layout. Large windows, massive fireplace, white carpeting. And lot of boxes. It reminded her of the time when her own dad had moved out.

"Don't be. Don't get me wrong. I wish our marriage wasn't ending, but I don't believe Gallivan the way my husband does."

"Believe him about what?" Angel asked, his voice quiet and strong.

Maggie's eyes reddened and her voice broke. "About . . . about Cory."

"Your son?" Buffy asked.

The woman looked at her sharply. "I didn't mention that I had a son."

"The real estate agent did," Buffy explained. "I told her about our own two kids." She avoided the glance Angel gave her. *Whoops! Forgot to tell him our cover story.*

"I know. When you mentioned you had kids, I knew I had to talk to you. Gallivan's people haven't told you about the other kids that have been kidnapped, have they?"

Willow walked beside Gallivan, following one of the sidewalk trails that cut through Weatherly Park. Oz trailed just behind her, close enough to take part in the conversation if he wanted to. So far, he was leaving it up to her.

Gallivan's bodyguards stayed alert, peering into the darkness. Willow had no doubt they carried weapons under their jackets. *I wonder if they have anything effective against vampires.* Remembering Buffy's reports she kept an eye on the shadows.

Rockett and his cameraman tried to follow, but Gallivan's security team had made that impossible. Craig and his wannabe freedom fighters had also been dissuaded.

"The security guy with the Campbells the other

night seemed to believe I was imagining things," Willow said. "But I know what I—"

"They're real," Gallivan interrupted. "Or rather, it's real. All I've ever heard of is one being seen at a time. Unless you saw more than that."

He believes me. He believes in this!

"No."

The industrialist hesitated just a moment and the behavior really stood out to Willow because he gave the impression of a guy who never hesitated. "What do you know about the lantern?" he asked.

"Lantern?" Willow shook her head. "I don't know anything about a lantern."

"I see. And you say you only saw one of the creatures." Gallivan sounded relieved. "Then maybe there's a way to contain this thing."

"Contain what?" Oz asked.

Gallivan stared at him as if trying to size him up. "All the bad publicity, of course."

Oz's face soured.

"Do you know what that thing is?" Willow asked.

"No."

"Ever had to deal with it before?" Oz tried.

"No," Gallivan said. "Never anything like it."

"The babies are being taken?" Willow asked. A chill ran through her as she realized for certain it was more than just Tad.

"So it appears."

"Then why aren't you going to the police?" Oz asked.

"You heard what she saw," Gallivan said. "What good are the police in this instance?"

Willow and Oz didn't comment. What good were the police in Sunnydale ever?

"As far as handing out speeding tickets, rousting the local juvenile delinquents, and containing the doughnut population," Gallivan said, "they're probably great. They're not, however, people I want to depend on. I'd rather depend on my own guys."

"What's happened to the babies?" Willow asked, desperate to stay on this point. An image of little Tad formed in her mind.

"I don't know. I've got people investigating. That's why I decided to talk to you."

"Me?"

Gallivan stopped in the middle of the concrete jogging path. His stance reminded Willow of an old-time gunfighter. "You're the first tie we've had between the disappearance of the children and direct opposition to the amusement park I want to build here."

Willow couldn't believe it. "You think I had something to do with it?"

"I don't know," Gallivan said. "That's what I thought I'd come ask you."

Willow was outraged. *I can't believe Gallivan thinks I had anything to do with this.* Anger and frustration took the place of most of the insecurities Willow had been feeling. "I didn't have anything to do with it!"

"The baby disappeared while you were there. Mrs. Campbell told me she put the boy to bed herself."

"*If* he was there," Willow said. "When I found that—that *thing,* it only looked like Baby Tad."

Gallivan's face wrinkled in perplexity. "What are you talking about?"

"That thing took the place of Baby Tad," Willow said. "It looked exactly like him till it accused me of not trying hard enough to stop you."

Doubt creased Gallivan's face. "Why would it want to stop me?"

"I don't know."

"And why choose you as its emissary?"

Because I'm a witch. "I don't know," she said aloud.

"You got a good look at the creature?"

"Yes."

"What was it?"

"The only thing I know for sure," Willow replied, "is that it's evil."

"Then I'm fighting something that's evil," Gallivan said. "Doesn't that make me on the side of good?"

The thought caused Willow to pause. Good and evil were two poles that had taken up residence in her life. She knew the world wasn't evenly or easily divided into the two camps, but sometimes it came close.

"Actually," Oz spoke up in his slow, thoughtful way, "it makes me think of that old saying about having to choose between the lesser of two evils. I don't think you're completely blameless in this. How many children are missing now?"

Pride filled Willow at Oz's insight.

Gallivan's face hardened. "That's privileged information."

"Yeah," Oz said, "but who's privileged by it? Families are missing their kids. They're obviously depending on you for help, only you're more interested in breaking ground on your amusement park."

"We all have our priorities," Gallivan said.

Seeing that Oz was on the verge of losing some of the cool that was so much his trademark, Willow interrupted. "Why did you want to talk to me?"

"I thought there was a chance we could come to some kind of agreement." Gallivan smiled. "This area is perfect for the amusement park my planning committee has developed. No other place in Sunnydale has quite the same access to the community and to the highways. However, I do have an opportunity to purchase another area that would make a fantastic open park that would replace this one in the community. I'm willing to finance the new park there and build the amusement center here."

"So you'll just buy us off?" Willow said.

Gallivan spread his hands, the winning smile tightly locked in. "That's what business is."

"This park," Willow said, "isn't business. It's memories and potential, and one of the truly beautiful places in Sunnydale." *If you don't count the vampires.*

"And I could find you another really nice park," the industrialist offered.

"No," Willow said. "We're going to be here and let people know what we're losing."

Gallivan nodded at his security people. "I think we're done here." He turned his attention back to Willow. "I wish we could have come to terms, Miss

Rosenberg, because I'm not going to be stopped. Not by your efforts, and not by this *creature* as you term it. I'm going to start with the people my security team caught last night. And if I can make the charges stick, I'm going to come after you for putting them up to it."

Fear clawed cat tracks up Willow's spine, prickling up her skin. She barely maintained eye contact with the industrialist, but Oz's being there, believing in her, made her stronger.

Gallivan turned and walked away, flanked by his bodyguards.

"What about the children?" Willow asked, starting after him.

"We'll find them," Gallivan threatened. "And whoever has them is going to pay."

"There's something you might consider," Oz said, jogging to keep up with Gallivan's stride. "Someone's trying to send you a message. If you don't get the message soon, whatever's taking the children may decide to come for you."

Gallivan stopped and gave them a hard look. "Is that supposed to be a threat?"

"No," Oz replied. "Just reminding you that you might want to watch your back."

"I pay somebody else to do that. And I'm far better protected than you people are."

CHAPTER 11

"Hector Gallivan's security people are keeping the kidnappings quiet," Maggie Chapin said.

Buffy listened, filling in the information she had only guessed at earlier. "How many kids?"

"Six that I know of," Maggie answered. "We lost Cory. I heard the Campbells lost their son Tad last night. The Englands lost both of theirs. The Moltons and the Dixons lost their daughters."

"The Englands lost two?" Buffy asked.

"Twin boys," Maggie said.

"How old?"

"Ten, eleven months. I forget."

"But less than a year old?" Angel asked, his hand tightening slightly on Buffy's arm.

Maggie nodded. Her eyes teared up and her voice thickened. "They all were. Just babies."

Maybe that's a clue, Buffy thought. According to

the faery legends Giles and Willow had discussed with them, the spriggans and other evil faeries always replaced babies. *Because they had power only over babies? Were they limited in some fashion?*

"That's terrible," Buffy said, acting like a concerned parent. It wasn't hard because it really was terrible.

"You look awfully young to have kids of any age. How old are they?" Maggie got up from her chair and walked to the fireplace mantel. She took a picture down.

"Four and two," Buffy replied. "We adopted." The lies felt bad now because Maggie was being so truthful with them.

"You might be safe. I've never heard of any kids over a year old being taken." Maggie handed Buffy the framed picture. "That's Cory."

Buffy studied the picture, imagining how it must feel not to see that smiling little face every day. "He's very cute." She handed the picture back. "I'm sorry."

Maggie took the picture and studied it. "He's still alive. A mother knows these things, you know."

Buffy nodded like she did know, not wanting to think of what she'd put her own mother through. "What is Gallivan doing about it?"

"He says he's got an army of private investigators on it. And he probably does. I talked to three of them myself. He thinks the children are being taken for blackmail. His corporation is very rich, as you know."

"But some of the parents don't believe that?" Buffy said.

"*I* don't believe that," Maggie said. "I may be the only one. Philip is like the other families Gallivan hired."

"They believe in Gallivan and the job is too good to risk," Angel surmised.

"Yes. Without the job, they'd have nothing. And it's only been a couple weeks since the first baby disappeared."

Two weeks? That was when the heavy machinery started breaking ground around Weatherly Park. Buffy shifted on the couch uneasily. "When did Cory disappear?"

Maggie's voice broke. "Eight days ago."

"Did you go to the police?"

She nodded. "That night. I was hysterical. I called them while Philip called Gallivan. We'd already found out one of the other babies was missing. Maybe two. Gallivan told Philip he'd take care of everything, and Gallivan wanted Philip to make sure I didn't talk to the police."

"But you did," Angel said, "because it only made sense to do that." His support of the decision was obvious, and Buffy knew it would reassure the woman. He was good with dealing with people.

"Yes. Philip tried to talk me out of it until they parked at the curb. I met them out in the yard. I didn't make a good impression, crying and screaming and yelling at Philip. He kept telling the police officers I'd had too much to drink at an office party."

"Had you been drinking?" Angel asked.

"No. But there was an office party Gallivan had hosted that evening at his estate here in Sunnydale. I didn't go, but Philip told them I had."

"So were you with Cory when he was taken or did you have a sitter?"

"No, I was there."

Buffy leaned in closer, deciding to risk the rapport she'd built with the woman. "You saw it, didn't you? The thing that took Cory?"

Tears ran down Maggie's surprised-looking face. "How do you know about that?"

"I haven't been entirely honest," Buffy admitted, feeling better now that she could tell more of the truth. "A friend of mine was baby-sitting at the Campbells' house last night when their son was taken."

"She saw the—the *thing?*"

"Yes."

"What did you see?" Angel asked softly.

Maggie looked at him, totally confused and distrustful. "Why should I tell you?"

Angel looked at the distraught mother. Buffy knew the intensity that dark gaze brought with it. Nobody could look at you the way Angel did.

"Because," he told her, "I know loss. And pain. And I want to spare anyone else what you've been through." He paused, letting the sincerity of his words sink in. "We're trying to find out what happened to the children. And if we do, we're going to try to bring them back."

"Do you think you can?" The hope in the woman's voice almost broke Buffy's heart and brought a lump to her throat.

Angel hesitated just a moment. "I don't know," he told her truthfully. "We're going to try."

Maggie tried to speak, couldn't, then tried again. "It was this little . . . horrid *thing*. That's all I know to call it. At first I thought it was Cory."

"But it changed," Angel said. "Didn't it?"

"Yes. It changed. It became something evil looking. It had wings, fangs, and these animal-like claws."

"Did it speak to you?" Buffy asked, leaning forward.

"Yes. I think that was the part that made Philip believe I was crazy. But it did talk. It told me to tell Gallivan to stop work on the forest. That the forest was under their protection."

"What happened to the thing?" Buffy asked.

"It flew away. I went to get Philip, and that was only minutes before I called the police. I told them too. That was when they really started believing Philip's story that I'd been drinking. Philip has always dealt with stress and turmoil better than I have. He was totally calm."

"That made what you were telling the police sound even worse," Angel said.

Buffy empathized with her, wondering how she'd managed to hang on this long. *But I guess you have to if you think you're going to need to be there for your child. I guess that's what keeps Mom dealing with everything she knows.*

Maggie nodded. "Philip told them that Cory was with a baby-sitter provided by Gallivan Industries for the party. They called the number he gave them, and someone told them Cory was there."

"But he wasn't?" Buffy asked.

"No, but the police didn't inquire further." She looked at them. "Do you really think you can help with this?" Her eyes held steady on Angel.

"Yes," he answered. "We've dealt with this kind of thing before." He reached forward and took her hands in his. "And we believe you, Maggie."

Buffy walked down the long dark street leading out of the Wingspread edition, a mixture of emotions swirling inside her. The mercury vapor lights painted her shadow long and lean before her, and she felt cold enough to wrap her arms around herself.

"You okay?" Angel asked.

"No," she answered honestly.

"That was kind of intense."

She blew out a long breath and glanced back, staring at the silhouette in one of the windows above the dead flowerbeds. "Yeah."

"So where to now?"

"Weatherly Park," Buffy said. "Until Giles or Willow can find something else for us to go on, the answer seems to be there." She picked up the pace, as if burning the extra energy would chase the confusion and borrowed pain from her. "And if we don't find the answer to this right away, at least the vampires will provide a distraction."

"Three cheeseburgers, a double order of fries, a jumbo chocolate shake, and two of those apple pie turnovers." Hutch turned from the Paco's Pastries counter in the mall's galleria. "What do you want, Xander? It's on me."

Xander glanced at his friend and shook his head doubtfully. "You sure you can afford to feed both of us?"

"Yeah," Hutch answered. "Today I can." He riffled the bills in his fist. "I've had a couple good weeks at the comic-shop. A guy came in and sold off his *X-Men* collection because he was getting married. Comics and wives, man, they just don't mix. Don't know how many guys I've seen give up their stuff when they get married."

Xander had a mini-nightmare of what it might be like to share a house with Cordelia. *How much stuff would I have to get rid of to meet her approval? What about my collection of . . .* He stopped himself before he got too far. *My life is never going to be someone else's ballast.* "Cheeseburger and a chocolate shake."

Hutch shook his head. "Don't see how you keep yourself alive. Hey," he addressed the guy working the counter, "where can I get me one of those paper hats? I mean, that's stylin'."

The clerk tried to shoot him a tough look.

Hutch only laughed uproariously. He paid and grabbed the tray when their order was completed.

"And I don't see where you put all that," Xander said, grabbing the shakes, wishing Hutch hadn't hassled the counter guy. The guy couldn't help it if he had a bad job with a dress code that totally sucked.

They found a table at the back of the food court between plastic palm trees in olive green buckets. Some thoughtful soul had sprayed the palm trees with pine air freshener, creating an interesting contrast of expectations.

"A couple of leis and we'd be right at home, huh?" Hutch asked, laughing in that big way of his.

They dug into the meal with gusto. Hutch had one of the cheeseburgers finished before Xander had taken two bites. "You ever count your fingers after you eat?" Xander asked, only halfway kidding.

Hutch grinned at him, then glanced out at the mall crowd going by. "Now there's a bad case of wishful thinking." He nodded toward a girl two sizes too big for the Spandex pants she wore.

Although he and Hutch shared the same skewed sense of humor and wit that had originally brought them together, Xander stopped short of being just pure mean. Xander didn't comment.

The mall crowd was in full swing, creating a steady buzz of conversation in pockets separated by neon lights and advertising. The walkers strode past, checking their heart rates with practiced proficiency, while the teens hung out in packs and talked big dreams. The mall, Xander had always felt, was where dreams and nightmares collided. Good and evil, success and failure—it was all there and not conveniently marked for consumption.

A few more minutes passed with conversation topics that ranged from comics to conspiracy theories to comics to the latest gag gifts they'd seen at the novelty store upstairs. Xander's attention wavered from Hutch, to the television above the Paco's Pastries booth, to his meal. Despite the discrepancy in volume, Hutch finished his cheeseburgers, fries, and drained his extra-large shake before Xander finished his. He polished off his apple turnovers while Xander finished his fries.

"Hey," Hutch said, "isn't that Willow?"

Xander followed Hutch's nod and looked at the television above Paco's Pastries. The local news station was carrying a live transmission from Weatherly Park. "That *is* Willow."

The story was short and brief, highlighting Willow's leadership in the protest against Gallivan Industries' efforts to build the new amusement park in Sunnydale.

"You know," Hutch said, "Willow is one hot babe. Saw that the other night when we went over to help her."

Cold apprehension threaded down Xander's spine. "Maybe you should lay off talking about Willow like that."

"Why? Hit a nerve?"

"She's a friend," Xander said with an unaccustomed edge in his voice. "Okay?"

Hutch shrugged. "Sure. Doesn't mean anything to me one way or the other."

That's not exactly what I wanted to hear either.
Xander tried to turn his attention back to his meal.

More footage, this provided from Gallivan's security people, rolled on the capture of the two Sunnydale high school students who'd been sabotaging the bulldozers used on the site. A few scenes of Gallivan himself after he spoke to Willow appeared. The reporters speculated that some kind of deal might be in the offing.

"Do you think Willow's going to knuckle under to this guy?" Hutch asked when the story finished.

Xander shook his head. "No."

"I don't know, man," Hutch said. "Willow doesn't seem to be the in-your-face type."

"She's not," Xander replied. "But she'll stick. You just don't know Willow. She's a believer, and when she believes in someone or something, she'll stick longer than anybody I know."

"Maybe," Hutch said doubtfully. "But you can bet Gallivan's not going to quietly go away." He paused. "Why aren't you out there with Willow?"

"You met Cordelia?"

Hutch nodded. "She doesn't approve of Willow trying to save the park?"

"The park doesn't appeal to Cordelia's sense of nowness," Xander explained. But he still felt guilty for not being there. Cordelia shouldn't make him feel he had to make a choice between them. Willow never did. "Maybe it would have been okay when she was a kid, but she's not one now."

Hutch grinned. "I've noticed."

"Don't notice so enthusiastically," Xander growled. *Sheesh, what is it with this guy and appetites?*

"Down, boy."

"Cordelia's afraid Willow's protests are going to sink the Spring Blow-Out. And the party is pretty much totaled."

"Nice to know Cordelia has her priorities," Hutch replied.

"Hey, you want to lighten up a little?"

"I'm just saying Willow seems to have the higher moral ground."

"You're looking for moral ground," Xander said, "but that turf's not for everybody. You're not exactly familiar with it yourself. I seem to recall a certain Spandex crudity from only a few minutes ago."

"I've never thought of myself as perfect."

"And I've never heard of you speak warmly of the park in these past weeks."

"I grew up here too," Hutch said softly.

"I didn't know that."

"There's a lot you don't know about me, Xander." Hutch was quiet for a moment, his gaze tracking over the menu at the fast-food counter again. "Gallivan might even get more desperate about the protest going on in the park."

"What do you mean?"

Hutch looked at him, his eyes flat and hard. "Willow's drawing a lot of attention to the land development deal. Usually any land set aside for parks and other community property is pretty well protected. Whatever legislation or agreement was originally defending that piece of land, however, seems to have disappeared in all the discussions."

"Not a pretty thought," Xander said.

"Didn't mean for it to be. At this point, you have to start wondering what kind of dirty deals Gallivan pulled off to even get the plans approved." Hutch paused. "And how far Gallivan's going to go to protect it. He's covering up the kidnapping of all those kids."

"So what made you Dick Tracy all of a sudden?"

"I was just thinking," Hutch said, "that it might be good to know more about Gallivan's business over there than what we do so far."

"Now that makes me feel kind of nervous and giddy," Xander said.

Hutch grinned, beating out a tune on the tabletop. "Me too. Exciting, isn't it?"

"Definitely. What do you have in mind?"

Hutch sprawled in the chair, finding more room for his long frame. "One of the regulars in the comics shop is a mall security guard. His company got hired to do some of the shift work at the park."

"I thought only Gallivan's staff were handling that."

"Not all the shifts, just the management and special projects. The guy told me that with all the protests going on, Gallivan Industries was thinking of putting more people on and it might mean a promotion for him."

"He gets a bigger badge or something?"

"He's hoping for a license to carry a gun."

"Now there's a cheery thought."

"Yeah," Hutch said in a way that let Xander know the idea was so *not*. "This guy loads up on *Sec Force, Full Auto,* and *The Penalizer*. He's deadly force just waiting to happen. I thought it might be a good idea to see what Gallivan's really hiding."

"How?" Xander asked, loving the hint of danger and illegality contained in Hutch's words.

As if by magic, Hutch opened his hand, revealing a small keyring. "While my guy was sorting through the back issues boxes when I offered him a special deal, I boosted his keys. The security company he works for has a small office in a building not far from here. I'm thinking Gallivan's such a control freak he's probably got his computers tied in somehow with the security company's system. With all the guards getting put on at the development site, there's nobody at the office. The watch commander's operating out of his car with a computer and a cell phone. Nobody's home."

Someone's given this a lot of thought, Xander thought. "So what do you plan on doing?"

"Letting myself into the office and taking a look at the computer system. I'm good with computers." Hutch closed his fist over the keyring. "You in or out?"

Xander thought about it for a moment. The immediate pull was the adrenaline rush, the same thing that made hanging with Buffy so cool. Another part was the fact that he'd kind of be spying on the corporate Goliath Willow was up against, and maybe even finding out key information they all needed.

"I'm in," he said.

"We'll be like Butch and Sundance," Hutch said, smiling.

"Maybe an analogy with a better ending would be more in order," Xander suggested. "I'm not into jinxing this little campaign before we get it off the ground."

"Pinky and the Brain?" Hutch asked, getting up from the table.

"No." Xander followed his friend through the food court.

"Yogi and Boo-Boo?"

"Never got a picnic basket did they?"

Hutch grinned.

CHAPTER 12

"That went well," Willow said, breathing a sigh of relief now that the protest had wrapped. She looked at Oz when confirmation wasn't immediately forthcoming. "Don't you think?"

He returned her gaze. "What? The part about let's all join together to save Weatherly Park, or the part about not firebombing the construction equipment because it would be a bad thing?"

Willow grimaced. "Okay. So maybe it didn't go so as well as it could have." She and Oz walked through the dark parking lot. A mosaic of shadows lay across the pavement, like a group of trapdoors just waiting to spring open.

The stragglers were just leaving. Most of them had been students, but there'd been a few more parents among them this time.

"Why do you think so many parents showed up tonight?" Willow asked.

Oz opened the passenger door of his van. "They were afraid all the phone lines at the police station would be jammed and they wouldn't get there with the bail money in time to keep their kids out of lockup with the real criminals."

"You're kidding . . . right?"

"Nope," Oz said. "At least, that's what I heard Jeannie Whitman's parents were here for."

"Jeannie wouldn't do anything." Willow got in.

Oz closed the door after her and looked in through the window. "As I recall, Jeannie was the one who offered to bring the bottles for the Molotov cocktails."

"Oh."

"Thought you heard that." Oz came around the van and got in.

"I must have missed it."

Oz slid behind the steering wheel and switched on the ignition. "You were kind of busy handling Craig at the time."

"Right." Craig had brought schematics for the various pieces of earth-moving equipment he'd downloaded from the Internet. He'd color-coded all the weak places where hydraulic fluid hoses could be cut that would keep them from operating. And he'd passed them out like candy at Halloween. "I'm not doing something wrong, am I?" she asked aloud. Indecision and insecurity ate at her sense of doing the right thing.

Oz shook his head, his attention on his driving.

"No, Will, I think if you do anything you believe in, you can't be doing wrong. As long as you don't cross over the line. You haven't."

Willow bit her lip. "Other people have because of it, though."

"There's always going to be people like that. You're not their keeper. It's enough for you to be responsible for your own actions."

"Even if they inspire someone else to cross that line?" *Where do you draw the line on personal responsibility?*

"Lance and Kelly *look* for lines to cross."

"Craig's not."

"Craig's looking for his first battle decoration."

Without warning, one of the visions filled Willow's mind. Baby Tad suddenly stood in the road ahead of them, dressed in his Mickey Mouse playsuit. "Stop!"

Oz stepped on the brakes at once. Rubber screeched as the van slid sideways. He looked at her, concerned. "What's wrong?"

Willow blinked her eyes. The image of Tad blurred, then evaporated. "I saw Tad again."

"Where?"

Willow pointed. "He was in the road." She dropped her hand to the door release and opened it. She was out of the van before Oz could stop her, drawn by the intensity of the vision. *What does it mean? Why am I getting these visions?*

There was only scarred pavement where she'd seen the baby.

"Are you okay?" Oz asked.

Willow trembled, feeling her knees go weak. "Yes. I think so. But I'm starting to wonder if I'm going crazy."

"If you have to wonder," Oz said gently, "then you're probably not in any danger."

"That was supposed to be funny, right?"

He shrugged and smiled at her lopsidedly. "Guess it wasn't, huh?" He touched her face tenderly. "You're going to be okay, Willow. I won't let you be any other way."

"I've got to find Tad," she told him, trying to make him understand how strongly she felt that.

"I know," he replied. "I know you do. You will. I'll help." He guided her gently back to the van. They were alone on the road, so when the rustling sounded above them, there weren't any other distractions.

Willow glanced up and saw three winged shapes land on the crooked branches overhead. Even though she couldn't see them clearly, she knew what they were. She grabbed Oz by the arm, no longer being led. She yanked him toward the van. "Run!" she ordered. "Run fast!"

Behind her, she heard wings beat the air as the faeries launched themselves from the trees.

"Hey, Buffy."

Crouched in the Stygian shadows crowded into all the small places of the park, Buffy heard the casual tone and thought the voice sounded familiar. She peered around the tree where she'd hidden.

The guy stepped into the clearing ahead of her wearing a Sunnydale High varsity jacket and khakis. His hair was shaved almost to the scalp, leaving only stubble behind. He looked young, but the hollow eyes had already set in.

"That's right, isn't it?" he asked, walking toward her slowly. "Buffy Summers. I always thought you looked so hot. Of course, that wasn't a cool opening line back in school."

"Back in school?" Buffy echoed, feeling pretty miserable about meeting him there. She stood up and hid the rough wooden stake behind her leg. "You were in school yesterday, Gary. Does it seem so long ago?"

Angel moved to her right through the trees, circling to provide cover for her. They'd already found and staked three vampires.

Gary carried a shovel in one hand, but he slapped the other one against his chest. "You remember me?"

"Second period," Buffy said. "You thought you were the class clown. It was kind of hard to miss you."

He laughed insanely, like she was a comedian. "I told people you'd be funny if they got a chance to get to know you."

Buffy stood and waited. "I'm not feeling very funny now."

"Maybe you don't get the joke." In the moonlight, he looked waxy and gaunt.

"What joke?"

"Knock knock."

"Who's there?" Buffy asked, letting him get closer.

"Dwayne."

"Dwayne who?"

Gary grinned. "Dwayne the blood bag. I'm starving." He laughed uproariously.

"Kind of like being a vampire, don't you?" Buffy asked, all sympathy for the guy leaving her.

"I would say it doesn't suck," Gary replied. "Except that it does." He bared his fangs. "Every chance it gets."

Before she could move, Buffy heard branches rattle overhead. She took a step back and glanced up, spotting the two vampires hanging upside down from the tree limbs overhead. They fell at her like missiles. Elongated fangs gleamed in their mouths.

Buffy leaped backward, going into a full somersault to get the most distance. One of them missed her, but the other crashed on top of her, knocking her to the ground.

The vampire was an older, heavier guy who looked like a truck driver. At least, he wore a Peterbilt cap and smelled like diesel, as well as the grave. He snarled and his face morphed somewhere between human and feral animal. He snapped at her and his teeth popped together only inches from her neck.

Buffy rolled and struggled to get away. She slapped the vampire in the face with her palm, putting as much of her weight behind the blow as she could and driving his head back as he snapped at her again.

His cold hand clamped around her throat, shutting off her breath. Trapped beneath his weight, she found it hard to fight him.

"You're out here looking for it, aren't you?" the truck driver vampire asked. "You heard about it too."

Freeing her empty hand, Buffy jabbed him in the eyes with her fingers.

He howled in pain and jerked back, one hand clamping over his eyes.

Buffy took advantage of his distraction. Pushing his weight to one side, she scrambled to the other and kicked out from under him. The other vampire came at her, cutting Gary off.

The second vampire was too confident. Buffy came up with him, lifting the stake before her. It crunched through just below his sternum, then she angled it up to his heart. He turned to ash and blew away.

The truck driver vampire howled and pushed himself up to his knees. He peered at her between his parted fingers. "Get her! Get her!"

Gary vaulted toward her, incredibly fast. His features morphed as he drew the shovel back over his shoulder. He set and swung it hard, swiping the blade at Buffy's face.

Reacting instantly, aware that Angel had run into other vampires in the trees beyond the clearing, Buffy kicked the shovel handle just behind the blade. The wood snapped with a loud crack and the shovel head went flying.

Totally surprised, Gary drew back the broken end of the shovel handle. "Wow. Who knew?"

"Me. And to tell you the truth, I think your comedy routine has come up a little stiff." Buffy grabbed the shovel handle and took it from him with a quick jerk. She reversed it in one hand, handling the length of wood as easily as a baton, then drove it into Gary's chest.

He grabbed the shovel handle sticking out of his chest and stared at it. "Ooh, now there's a fatality move." Without another word, he exploded into dust.

The truck driver tried to get to his feet. Buffy drove a spinning back kick into his face and knocked him down again. He rolled, spitting and snarling, his claws raking the ground.

Buffy kicked again but missed. Before she could recover, the vampire got to his feet and punched her. She flew backward and landed on the ground with a bone-jarring thump. As she got to her feet again, the vampire rushed her, arms spread and yelling some kind of rebel yell thing.

Setting herself, Buffy grabbed the lapels of his denim shirt and halted his headlong charge by kicking him in the stomach and doubling him over. While he was doubled over, she brought her knee up three times in rapid succession, slamming it into the vampire's face.

As he staggered back, Buffy shoved him with one hand. She seized a stake from her bag with the other. She didn't stop pushing him till he flattened up against a tree. She dropped the point of the stake against his chest and stared into his dead eyes.

"How lucky do you feel now, gruesome?" she asked. "I mean, with the stakes raised?"

He stared at her with sour sullenness.

Buffy raised her voice, aware that sounds of a struggle no longer came from the nearby brush. "Angel?"

"I'm here." Angel strode into the clearing and brushed leaves from his clothing. "Two more are down."

"Traitor," the truck driver vampire hissed at Angel.

"Are you saving him for anything special?" Angel asked coldly.

"I think he knows what they're looking for," Buffy answered. She looked the vampire in the eyes. "Don't you?"

"Maybe."

"And you're going to tell us," Buffy promised.

"Let me go if I do?"

"Hmm, let me think . . . no."

The vampire trucker didn't seem surprised by the answer. "Then there's no reason to tell you."

Buffy wrinkled her brow as if trying to make a decision. "Staked or parboiled at dawn? *Staked* or *boiled.*" She shook her head. "There's just no way to make that sound nice, is there?"

"You wouldn't do that."

"Yes," Buffy lied. "I would."

Angel took a small metal Thermos from his jacket

pocket. "Holy water," he said quietly. "It'd be interesting to see how fast your toes burn off." He shook the Thermos threateningly. "And if you've heard of me at all, you know I'll do it."

A defeated expression filled the vampire's face. "Rumor has it there's some kind of leprechauns or faeries living in the forest. All this excavation around here has made them come out into the open again. We didn't know they existed."

"What does that have to do with the vampires?" Buffy asked.

"Legend has it that if a vampire finds the home of the leprechauns, he gets one wish granted."

"I've never heard that," Angel said.

The trucker vampire shrugged. "You're not from around here, are you, boy? At least, not originally."

"No." The disbelief continued to resound in Angel's voice.

"That story's been around here a hundred and fifty years," the vampire said. "I know because I've lived every one of them. And I think I'll live a few more!" He twisted suddenly, breaking free of Buffy's stranglehold. Quick on his feet and totally desperate, he almost made the safety of the underbrush.

Spinning, Buffy drew the stake back, then hurled it forward. The stake flipped and caught the fleeing vampire between the shoulder blades. He turned to dust while leaping for cover.

"They're out here because of superstition," Angel said.

"You think that's all it is?" Buffy asked.

"C'mon," Angel said. "You can't believe that drivel."

Buffy looked at him, noticing how the shadows around them altered the planes of his face. She tried hard not to think of how handsome a face it was. "Some people still think vampires are myths. Zombies. Werewolves. Ghosts. And if somebody had told me about the Slayer a few years ago, I wouldn't have believed that either. We're living in the DMZ of superstitions and myths. Maybe they're wrong, but now we know what they're out here for."

"We've staked eight vampires tonight," Angel said. "But you know we've seen at least a couple dozen more. It's going to be hard to get rid of all of them by the Spring Blow-Out." He glanced at the woods where he'd come from. "Two of those guys were security guards taken in the last couple days."

"Gallivan's not reporting that either."

"Surprise."

"Not," Buffy agreed. "Gary was at school yesterday, I think, and a vampire tonight. This is getting out of hand." She picked up her backpack and slung it over one shoulder.

"There's only one way to get rid of them here," Angel said.

"Find out how to clear the faeries," Buffy said. "I know. Giles is working on it, and Willow is closer to them than anyone thinks."

A shrill scream suddenly cut through the forest around them.

Buffy tracked the direction automatically, swinging around. Then she realized she knew the voice. "That was Willow!"

Angel nodded and raced in the direction of the scream with all the incredible speed his vampire powers gave him. Buffy stayed at his side, her own Slayer prowess and adrenaline surge giving her as much speed as he had. They plunged through the night-black forest, breaking branches and ripping through brush.

Please, pleasepleaseplease don't let me be too late . . .

Getting into the office building where Baxter Security was located proved relatively worry-free. Xander trailed after Hutch, surprised how lightly the big guy moved on his feet.

Baxter Security was on the third floor, Suite 310. The carpet was worn thin, advertising a lack of real prosperity. *Don't know if it's because the security guards in Sunnydale get such a bad rep, or if it's because it's not exactly a growth industry. With so much weirdness going on all the time, they have about the same survival rate as Starfleet red shirts.*

Hutch paused in the dimly lit hallway before the door to Suite 310. The glass windows displayed office hours, a brief advertisement, and two phone numbers in white letters.

Xander peered through the window shade and saw a simple desk and phone set up on the other side on the left. A half-dozen mismatched chairs lined the wall to the right. A bronze-colored door with a nameplate on it hung on the back wall. Xander reached down and tried the door, finding it locked.

"Careful," Hutch said. "We don't want to set off any alarms."

Xander nodded and stepped back. At the mall, the idea of invading Baxter Security offices in the hopes of accessing a way into Gallivan Industries' mainframes had sounded totally rad. Now, standing in front of the door and knowing they could get so busted, it sent a cold chill through him. *You don't exactly get to meet the best of people in lockdown.*

"Maybe this isn't such a good idea," Xander said, trying to sound cool about it.

"Weenieing out on me?" Hutch taunted. He knelt in front of the door and reached into his jacket pocket, bringing out an aerosol spray can.

"No," Xander said. *But it wouldn't take much. This is really a bad idea now that I think about it.* "Since it's locked, are you going to settle for some obnoxious graffiti?"

"We're getting in," Hutch said. He inserted a small plastic nozzle straw onto the spray can. Fitting the nozzle into the lock, he pressed the valve. The spray can sounded as loud as a 727 taking off in the hallway.

Xander glanced around nervously, knowing someone was going to come investigate at any second. Only they didn't, and in the next minute Hutch swung the door open.

"Coming?" Hutch gestured toward the open door.

"Yeah."

Xander reluctantly went inside, peering around at the sides. "What was in the can?"

"Graphite. Causes cheap tumblers to slip right through themselves."

"And you learned that where?" Xander entered the room, growing braver because it looked like they were going to get away with it.

"Latest issue of *ArachniKid*. Don't you stay current?"

"A guy with eight arms and no social life isn't a staple in my reading routine," Xander admitted. *Eight arms might be different, but the no-social-life is too close to home.*

Hutch came in and shut the door behind them.

"Computer," Xander said, pointing to the one on the secretary's desk.

Hutch shook his head. "They wouldn't keep it here. The guy that comes in the store says his boss is one of those real self-important types. It'll be there." He went to the door to the back office and ripped the lock out with a screech.

"I suppose there's a reason you didn't graphite that door too," Xander said. *Hutch is getting way too into this.*

"Sure," Hutch said. "What fun is it breaking into a place if you don't let them know you were there?"

"I really wouldn't know."

"Trust me," Hutch said. "It's not the same." He pushed the door and walked through. "Oh man, this guy has got a major obsession."

Xander stepped into the office and saw it was covered with photos from different crime scenes. He was really getting concerned till he saw some of the police vehicles pictured were from different towns and even states. It was just a hodgepodge of pictures of law enforcement in action. *Maybe it impresses the clients,* Xander thought. *Or maybe this guy gets one of those feel-good sweats out of looking at the police force in action shots.*

Hutch took the high-backed chair behind the desk. He cracked his knuckles theatrically, then tapped the keyboard experimentally. "Okay, let's see what you've got there, Brainiac."

Xander peered at the screen. Even though he was used to the miracles Willow seemed able to pull out of a computer, those feats paled in comparison to the skill Hutch seemed to wield. For the first time, Xander got a really good look at Hutch's hands. "Hey, your forefingers are longer than your middle finger." And they were. By about half an inch.

Hutch made pistols of them and shot Xander, then blew off the "barrels." "Better for pointing, Grandma. You trying to say I'm deformed or something?"

Xander shook his head. "Not me."

"I hate it when people do that." Hutch reached in his pocket and took out a package of M&Ms. He opened it and started crunching away. He offered the package to Xander. "Want some?"

Xander held up a hand in surrender. "Pass. Still full from Paco's Pastries." He watched Hutch at work.

"Good," Hutch said triumphantly, "he's got a dial-up link to Gallivan Industries. Once I get past their firewalls and security programs, we're going to be home free."

Xander watched and tried not to act like he was on the verge of a nervous breakdown. *If a silent alarm gets tripped, does that mean we don't hear it in here either?* It wasn't a happy thought.

CHAPTER 13

"Rupert," the deep voice on the other end of the phone line said. "So nice to hear from you."

"Desmond," Giles said, wiping his hands on the apron he wore. He peeled the garment off and laid it on the counter of the small bachelor's apartment he kept not far from the high school. He turned the stove burners off and put his meal to one side. Over the years of preparing to become a Watcher and actually handling that position with Buffy, he'd learned meals had to be things that could be put off and taken back up again.

"But, if I know you, this is a business call."

"Actually, yes it is." Giles paced the small living room. "Have you had a chance to look at that document I faxed to you?"

"Of course, my friend, otherwise I wouldn't be troubling you so late."

"It's later where you are, my friend. Or earlier I suppose, depending on your point of view."

"*Da,* and these old bones creak more than they used to."

"I think you have a few more good years in you yet," Giles said. Desmond Tretsky was something over ninety years old and showed no signs of stopping.

"Thank you for the vote of confidence, but the winter years have been kind to me. This note is interesting. So full of portent. Have you had a chance to read any of it?"

"I've got the gist of it. Things appear to be somewhat sticky."

"In this profession, there are no other circumstances. You live life at its keenest edge, and usually with only your own razor-sharp wits to keep you clear."

"There is also the Slayer."

"Ah, dear Rupert, always you espouse the worth of those we're destined to train. But how many ever really get seasoned enough to truly contribute to their own perilous salvation, save for the physical skills they're given upon reaching their station?"

Giles refused to rise to the offered bait. He and Desmond, though deepest friends in other respects, held firmly to disparate beliefs in the Slayer's role. "She's quite good, you know."

"Yes, and I trust that you'll train her well during the time you have with her."

Quietly frustrated, knowing Desmond was deliberately reminding him of the sometimes brief tenure a Watcher had, Giles rubbed the back of his neck. He knew Desmond was resentful of the fact his own Slayer, whom he'd spent several years with, had died never having had the chance of demonstrating the education Desmond had provided.

"This research is quite fascinating," Giles said, hoping to steer the conversation onto more positive ground.

"Faeries, as you know, are not unknown to our group."

"Yes, I was well aware of that."

"Have you had any experience with them yourself?"

"No." Giles's experiences had been many and varied, and not always ones condoned by his own mentors. A familiarity with a subject bred a certain rebelliousness as well. He'd raised his own demons, physically on occasion, and dealt with them.

"Most, as you'll discover," Desmond said, "are quite treacherous. They lie. They steal. Several of the different races are quite frankly homicidal."

"As is this one we're currently facing."

"Yes. Though in actuality, this group of them shouldn't be any problem of yours."

"We're still deciding on the extent of that," Giles said. "Though their activity has certainly embraced one of the people on Buffy's periphery."

"My advice on the matter would be to steer clear of them," Desmond said. "These are very bad things, my friend, and can possibly cause you tragedy in the long run."

"I understand that," Giles said, getting upset about Desmond's long way around to the point. "I'll certainly take that under advisement."

"You'd do well if you did. Let's talk about your faeries in particular, shall we?"

"Yes."

"The narrative you found at the excavation site came from a Russian trapper who was managing a fur trading outpost of the northwestern sector of the United States. He was the one who first came across the lantern after it arrived here, and the history that goes with it."

"What lantern?" Giles asked.

"Some of this is only intimated in the narrative, not fully explained because the narrator didn't have the whole story. He lived among the Indians, you see, buying and selling furs along the Pacific Northwest for Russian clothiers. He'd done a fair bit of trapping himself in that area, and sometimes traveled with his teams down to San Francisco when areas in the north were thought to be impassable. Dmitri, the man who wrote the narrative, arrived in San Francisco only a few years after the Gold Rush at Sutter's Mill."

Giles made notes to support his memory. Shorthand chicken scratches, actually.

"In San Francisco," Desmond continued, "Dmitri spotted the lantern hanging on a tavern. He didn't know what it was at first, but after examining it, he knew it was of Russian origin."

"By the design?" Giles asked. "I think that's a stretch there."

"By the writing on it," Desmond said. "The markings were in Russian script. The tavern owner had thought the lantern rather decorative and had replicas made. Remember, those times were filled with largesse from the gold strikes. When Dmitri read what was on one of the lanterns, he was moved to find the original lantern. For the moment, we'll go a little further back in time."

Despite the immediate fear the flying faeries caused in her, Willow kept her head. Her heart pounded frantically in her chest.

"Get down!" Oz yelled at her side. He struggled out of his jacket as he ran with her. Moving quickly, he flung the jacket up, netting a foot-and-a-half-tall faery with a stone axe about to swing at Willow.

The jacket wrapped around the flying creature, trapping it. It dropped from the sky and thudded against the ground. The tiny voice squeaked curses. Small hands and feet worked against the material.

Miniature arrows filled the air around Willow. She covered her head with her hands and kept running. Oz streaked at her side. The sharp arrowheads embedded in the pavement, stabbing up at an angle. Willow ran through them, snapping the delicate shafts.

"Willow!" one of the creatures shouted out behind her.

She ignored it, glancing at Oz to make sure he was still there. The van was only a few feet away when she saw the arrow strike him in the back of his neck. It quivered when it struck home. Almost immediately, Oz tripped over one of the faeries that had flown beneath him and he fell.

"Oz!" Willow stopped and turned toward him. The faeries filled the air above her, thick as a swarm of bees. The moonlight glittered with razor-edged silver around her. She grabbed Oz by the arm, feeling him kick and tremble. "Oz!"

"Go!" he ordered her in a weak voice. "Get out of here!" He tried to get up again, but wound up only sprawled out a little further than he had been.

Willow pulled desperately on his arm. *I'm not going to leave you, Oz. You wouldn't leave me, and there's no way I could do that to you.* He looked up at her and tried to pull his arm from her grip, but he was too weak.

Then Oz's eyes rolled up into his head and he went completely limp.

Willow couldn't tell if he was breathing. She called out his name frantically, pulling at him, but she wasn't strong enough to do more than drag him. The faeries surrounded her, the air filled with the hum of their beating wings.

"You must come with us, Willow," the faery in front of her said.

"No. Leave me alone." She refused to let go of Oz and pulled on him as hard as she could. His dead weight slid only a few inches.

"Don't you want to save the children?" the faery taunted.

"You won't let me," Willow said in frustration. *Oh, Oz, please be okay. Please wake up.*

"You can't leave, Willow. You will save the forest. You will save us." The faery reached into his bag and flung a handful of glowing dust into her face.

Willow fought against it, trying not to breathe in. But the dust touched her eyes and was absorbed into her skin. Lethargy stole her senses and drank down her mind in a long gulp. She saw the pavement coming up, but she never felt it hit.

"The original lantern was crafted in Russia," Desmond was saying. "I got this story from a colleague within my circle, who was able to research the story he translated. A landed family in Russia, one of the czar's nobility who'd fallen out of favor with the courts for taking part in an insurrection bid, was forced to flee St. Petersburg upon threat of death."

"Now there's an invitation you can't find at the card store," Giles commented dryly.

"True," Desmond said. "This family was reputed to have wealth and favor because of the domovoi that looked out for them. The legend says that one of the patriarchs of the family helped a faery king by the name of Elanaloral some years in the past and won his undying gratitude."

"How?"

"One of the legends that I turned up in my own research indicated that Elanaloral's own rise to head of state among the faeries was due to the family's aid in destroying one of his rivals. Using his powers, the faery king helped provide the man and his family after him with wealth and power. It's believed that had the head of the family left Elanaloral alone, the family might have become the rulers of Russia. However, he didn't have the patience for that. He wanted the power and wasn't content to let it pass to some future family member. The man grew ambitious and tried to stage a coup. He was sentenced to death. Even with the help of the faeries, he narrowly escaped with his life. The czar's soldiers pursued him to the coast, where he bought passage for his family on a ship bound for the western colonies."

"To California?"

"Actually," Desmond said, "it's believed they were headed for Alaska. Russian communities were starting to flourish there because of the fur trade. In Sitka and other places. The man gathered all of Elanaloral's people to him, knowing they couldn't risk the domovoi being discovered. Using the generosity of the faery against them, the man had the faery king bind his people with a magical spell. It took days of them hiding and running, and sometimes fighting to reach the coast and the ship. When it was finished, King Elanaloral and his people were imprisoned in a lantern, making it easier for them to be transported."

"This is the lantern Dmitri found on the San Francisco tavern," Giles said.

"*Da.* The man got passage for himself and his family aboard a ship and set sail. Unfortunately, as did happen in those days, the ship didn't complete the voyage. It sank somewhere off the California coastline, the victim of a harsh storm. When Dmitri talked to the tavern owner, he discovered that the lantern had been one of the few surviving items aboard a shipwreck that washed up on the shores near the city a handful of years before. Normally, most metals dissolve in the sea, giving in to the harsh bite of the salt and other elements. Gold and platinum, however, do happen to survive."

"This tavern owner didn't recognize the lantern as gold?" Giles asked.

"It was platinum," Desmond answered. "And apparently the tavern keeper thought it was silver, which was nearly worthless in a gold-bearing country. He liked the lantern so much he had the replicas made. After he was told of the lantern's history, Dmitri was certain this was the lantern of those legends."

"So why was it so interesting to him?" Giles asked.

"It was reputed to have special powers," Desmond answered. "It was supposed to be capable of preventing diseases and death and of delivering great power. All the things a man in those days would go searching for."

"Or in this day, as a matter of fact," Giles said. He was beginning to get a really bad feeling about the lantern. "So what was inside the lantern?"

"The legends that were referenced don't say. Perhaps some otherworldly pocket universe. Perhaps nothing at all. Whatever it was, it eventually drove the faery king and his subjects quite mad when they were trapped inside."

"Mad?" Giles's stomach flip-flopped.

Buffy broke through the ragged treeline two steps ahead of Angel. They didn't try to go quietly, instead pounding through the silence that seemed to vibrate around them. Willow's scream had died away seconds ago. Turning left, Buffy spotted Oz's van stopped in the middle of the road. She ran for it at once, staying next to the treeline.

A dense group of what looked like soap bubbles hung in the air above Oz. He lay on the ground, arms and legs fanned out around him.

"Oz!" Buffy yelled. She ran toward him, looking around wildly. Willow was nowhere to be seen.

The glimmering soap bubbles burst apart. They formed tendrils that flowed toward Buffy. As they got closer, she recognized the gleams as the wings of faeries. She also noticed that some of the reflections came from the weapons they carried. She called out a warning to Angel and set herself into a defensive position.

The lead faery carried a small, incredibly sharp sword that fit its hand perfectly. The blade swiped at Buffy's head.

She ducked beneath the blow and came up with a front-snap kick that caught the faery dead center. The creature flipped backward, its wings slapping at the air frantically. Still in motion, she continued her attack, kicking and punching two more faeries that came at her.

Angel was in motion only a few steps away. He used the long tails of his jacket as well as his hands to combat the flying faeries. They shrieked and screeched in their high-pitched voices, snapping their wings and trying to find room to maneuver.

Buffy found it easier to push toward the masses of faeries rather than try to take them on one to one. They couldn't move well in groups and they interfered with each other. She reached Oz and stood guard over him, staring helplessly at the small arrow in the back of his neck.

An arrow ripped through the air and passed through her hair, narrowly missing her face. She stepped forward and kicked, bringing her foot down on the faery. It screamed in pain, thudding against the pavement a few times before it was able to take to the air again.

She tried to remember everything that Willow and Giles had said about faeries that morning, searching for a weakness she could use against them. *Iron,* she remembered Giles saying. *Good to know, but I don't have any with me.* She kept fighting, keeping them away from Oz.

One faery reached into a small satchel at its side. Flying close to her, it flung a handful of glowing dust at her. Buffy stepped back, avoiding the dust cloud by doing a back flip, taking out two more faeries with kicks. She breathed deeply, keeping the oxygen flowing through her blood. She didn't warn Angel because he didn't breathe anyway.

The faeries hung back, more cautious now. They

regrouped, giving each other more room. Another dozen buzzed away from Angel. No casualties. Every faery that had been hit had recovered.

Four arrows flew at Buffy. She dodged away, flipping toward the treeline. She flipped again and came down on her feet, and then stepped into the shelter of the branches. Glancing down at the ground, she chose a half-dozen smooth stones that were just the right size. Holding them in her left hand, she stepped back out of the treeline as the faeries hovered nervously.

She tossed the stones like throwing stars, whirling them into the faeries with uncanny accuracy. They hit the winged creatures with enough impact to knock them backward. Then one of them called the retreat. They flapped their wings, leaving the area en masse.

Buffy threw herself in pursuit, trying desperately to keep up. Willow hadn't been at the scene, but Buffy knew Willow had been with Oz. He wouldn't have left without her. But even her own speed didn't allow her to keep up. The faeries disappeared in seconds. She turned and found Angel behind her.

"They got away," Buffy said disgustedly.

"They didn't get far," Angel told her. "We'll find them, and we'll find Willow."

Buffy nodded, then led the way back to the road. She knelt beside Oz, gently rolling him over.

He blinked his eyes and looked up at her. "Willow?" he croaked, worry filling his eyes.

Buffy hesitated, not wanting to tell Oz the bad news.

"They got her," Angel told him softly, dropping a hand on Oz's shoulder. "But we're going to get her back."

Oz nodded weakly. "She said she saw the baby. Tad. That's why we stopped."

"It's going to be okay," Buffy promised. "We'll call Giles and Xander, and we're going after her. Let's get to a phone." She pulled him to his feet.

CHAPTER 14

"The faeries went mad," Giles repeated, underlining the word on his notepad. "As in insane?"

"Mad as in terribly insane, according to Dmitri," Desmond answered. "The Russian managed to isolate the real lantern, then stole it from the tavern and fled. Evidently the tavern owner wouldn't sell it to him."

"How did Dmitri end up here in Sunnydale?"

"He was familiar with the Indian tribe the local archeologists are only now starting to excavate," Desmond answered. "Dmitri had stayed among them before during his trading trips and was welcomed by their tribe. While he was there, he solved the riddle of the lantern, managing to undo the spell that held the faeries trapped."

"He freed them?"

"Only a few of them," Desmond said. "The exact

answer isn't given in the narrative, but it was enough to convince Dmitri they were uncontrollable. However, those few sought out other supernatural creatures in the area to help them try to free the rest of their band. Notably, the vampires. The faeries no longer trusted humans for the most part, and they made a deal with some of the vampires in the area. In exchange, the faeries had protected the vampires, kept them from harm. If a protected vampire was slain, the faeries gathered its dust and resurrected it with their magic. Unfortunately, as with most beings that come into sudden and easy power—"

"The vampires got greedy," Giles interposed.

"As did the freed faeries. They attacked the Indian village and tried to take the lantern and the rest of their people. The vampires weren't successful in combating the Indians, but the attack did pique the chief's interest in the lantern Dmitri insisted they protect. As a result of his people getting killed by the vampires, and the fact that they had to stake a few of them later who returned from death, the chief took the lantern from Dmitri. Our records end there, leading us to believe it might be there at the excavation site."

"What happened to Dmitri?" Giles asked.

"He was blamed for the attack on the tribe," Desmond said. "And he was driven from their camp. After discovering the existence of the faeries inside the lantern, the chief struck a deal with King Elanaloral. In exchange for his people's release from the lantern's spell, the faery king agreed to protect the Indians and the forest, never allowing their enemies to despoil it."

"But the Indians were killed."

"Eventually," Desmond agreed. "Although the preliminary excavations done by the local archeologists seem to indicate the tribe succumbed to inner strife that decreased their numbers and to a disease that finally wiped them out one harsh winter."

Giles flipped open the notepad to the place where he'd taken notes from Willow's recitation of the Campbell baby kidnapping. "What about something called the Homestone?"

"Ah, the Homestone," Desmond said, "this is where things begin to get even more interesting again . . ."

The ease Hutch showed at slicing through Gallivan Industries' computer security stunned Xander. He peered over his friend's shoulder, listening to the syncopation Hutch drummed into the keyboard.

Screen after screen of names, numbers, and video flashed by. The interrupts between sites within the corporation grew longer with each new entry as the defensive programming fought his progress. And Xander got uneasier with each one.

"What are you looking for?" Xander asked, speaking barely above a whisper.

Hutch's fingers never hesitated. "Just looking."

"You act like a guy who's looking for something in particular."

Hutch grinned. "And what would you be looking for if you were doing the looking?"

"Maybe a list of names of the babies who're missing," Xander said, shrugging. "Some of the details of Gallivan's security people's efforts to get them back."

"Got the list of babies first," Hutch said. "It's on the floppy disk. And I've just penetrated the security files. I'm breaking the encryption on the search effort now."

Xander watched as screens continued to flash by. Every now and then he caught a word and sometimes a whole phrase. The sixth sense warning him of when events around him were definitely not right flared up. Not enough to trigger the fight or flight response like facing a vampire would, but enough that he couldn't ignore it.

"They've been searching the forest," Hutch interrupted his thoughts. "I'm pulling down topographical maps, geological maps, and aerial photos of the forest and park now."

"Gallivan's security people are looking for them there?" Xander asked.

"Yeah," Hutch replied. "Looking for the missing kids—as well as other things."

"What other things?"

"Caverns. Tunnels. Old sites of past cities and cultures."

"Like an Indian village?"

"Yeah." A troubled look appeared on Hutch's face. "The lantern. They're looking for the lantern!"

"What lantern?" Xander asked.

Hutch seemed hesitant just a moment, then he

shook his head. "I don't know. There's just a notation here about a lantern."

"Why would Gallivan be interested in anything like that?"

"It doesn't say here. Maybe you could ask him."

"Right."

Suddenly, the computer screen went black. "The sysop discovered me," Hutch said. He started banging away at the keys with even greater speed. "He's trying to ferret me out."

"Then let's haul," Xander said. "We've got something to work with. That's more than we came with."

"No," Hutch said. "I only need a little more. The location's there. I know it is."

"What location?" Xander shifted nervously. "C'mon, Hutch, if Gallivan's computer security has made us, it's time to be a rolling stone."

"It's there." Hutch battled the keyboard in a frenzy that was almost superhuman. Abruptly, the screen cleared, revealing a series of maps. Hutch smiled broadly. "Yeah! Got it!"

"Got what?"

"What I was looking for, Xander."

"Maybe I'm thinking about this all wrong," Xander said, turning back from the door, "but I was under the impression this was a joint effort."

"It is," Hutch said. "It's just that parts of it are more joint than others." He pressed the eject button on the floppy drive and kicked the disk free. He palmed it, then tucked it inside his shirt pocket. "Let's bail." He passed Xander, heading for the door to the outer office.

Noticing the folder Hutch had highlighted on the hard drive, Xander shoved another disk into the drive and copied the folder. It copied in seconds. He popped it free and started after Hutch just as a flashlight beam cut the darkness in the hallway. *Hutch, ol' buddy, your interest in this whole thing seems to have progressed* way *beyond the let's-hack-the-world motivation. Time to see what's what.*

Xander shoved the disk into his pants pocket and hastily moved to Hutch's side. The spitting crackle of a walkie-talkie echoed in the hall.

Hutch paused at the door and peered out. Xander joined him, looking down the corridor and spotting the two security guards shining flashlights on both sides of the corridor, shaking doors as they came to them. Before he could move, one of the flashlight beams nailed him against the door to the security office.

"There!" one of the guards yelled.

"Hey, you," the other one roared, "stop!"

Now there's a plan, Xander thought. *Not!* He pushed himself forward down the hall, diving out of the light. Hutch was up ahead of him, running for all he was worth.

"C'mon!" Hutch yelled. He slammed through the stairwell and held the door open. Xander was at his heels, yet Hutch still managed to be the first one down the stairs. Xander rebounded off the walls of the next landing, bouncing back on track.

Each drawn breath burned Xander's throat. Hutch was at least fifty pounds heavier than he was, but he actually lost ground in the race. Alarms rang out behind them now, echoing up and down the stairwell.

On the first-floor landing, Hutch shoved through the fire doors again, and stepped into the bright lights of more guards' flashlights. He filled the doorway, letting Xander fade back into the stairwell. Another stairwell led on down into the basement. He stayed by the door, stopping himself short before calling Hutch. *Man, how did I let him talk me into this? Getting caught is not acceptable.*

Growing antsy, Xander made himself remain still, listening to the footsteps of the guards from above thundering down toward him. He wanted to call out to Hutch but didn't. *It won't do any good if we're both caught.* Reluctantly, he stepped back from the door but couldn't help watching what was going on outside.

Hutch froze when the security guards ordered him to. He feinted to the left and the guards followed the move, trying to block his way to the door. Hutch swiveled right, letting go of the door and stepping into the shadow, out of sight of the guards.

The guards swung their lights toward the new position. Only, when the lights hit the wall and floor, Hutch was gone.

Xander couldn't believe it, scanning the area but finding no sign of his friend. For a moment, he was frozen, listening to the guards as they talked over their walkie-talkies. Then the fire door swung shut. Xander ducked down into the basement garage.

He ran across the garage, dodging between the cars. A sliver of light shone through the closing door as he went into hiding. He reached the public entrance on the other side of the garage, tossing a nonchalant wave to the parking attendant.

Outside, he turned left and raced down the block. He spotted Hutch's car, watching as the engine caught and it drove away.

Glancing around, Xander spotted the convenience store across the street. He bolted for it just as a security guard stepped outside the building's main entrance. Inside, he called Buffy from the payphone, but her mom said she wasn't there. Giles's phone number netted only the answering machine. He skipped leaving a message, guessing that something was up.

He tried Cordy's phone next and caught her on her way out the door. "Hey, Cordelia, it's Xander."

"Where are you?" she demanded. "Buffy just called. Willow's been taken by the faeries. I'm on my way to the park now."

The news hit Xander like a sledgehammer in the stomach. He looked at the rows of chips, peanuts, and candies and tried miserably to pretend everything was still normal. "I need a lift," he said. "I got stranded." He took the floppy disk from his pocket and looked at it. "And we'll need to stop by Willow's to get her laptop computer. I think I've got one of the pieces of this puzzle."

And Hutch's unexpected and unexplained disappearance at the security office dropped another piece into place. *Elongated fingers, an incredible appetite, and a mean sense of humor. Gotta be.*

* * *

"Giles is there." Oz pointed from behind the driver's seat of his van.

Buffy glanced across the street and saw the Watcher's small car parked near the outside payphone at the small mom-and-pop all-night grocery only a few blocks from Weatherly Park. They'd decided to meet there to make a game plan before going out to the park.

Pulling on the steering wheel, Oz cut into the parking lot, barely edging out an SUV that definitely didn't fit the neighborhood profile. He tapped the brakes and brought them to a rocking stop.

Buffy retreated to the vehicle's rear long enough to grab the weapons she'd selected for the night.

Giles spotted her and came across at once. He carried a weather-beaten leather valise under one arm. He looked grim.

"Buffy," he greeted. "Xander and Cordelia have also joined us. I'm afraid the matter is somewhat more grave than I'd even thought when we discussed it over the phone."

Buffy hoisted the canvas duffel bag over her shoulder and glanced at Xander and Cordelia, who were moving out of the shadows.

"Okay," she said, drawing a breath, "let me know how bad it is. On a scale of one to ten, with one being wearing the same prom dress as a dozen other girls and ten being something short of plastic surgery that leaves you looking ready for a *Twilight Zone* episode."

"I had the document we found at the excavation

site analyzed and interpreted," Giles pressed on. "We *are* dealing with faeries."

"Giles, they have wings, bad attitudes, throw sleep dust, and carry Micro-Machine–sized weapons," Buffy said. *"Timmy* could have gotten that one *without* Lassie barking in his ear."

"The kind of faeries is interesting." Giles remained totally unflappable in that British way of his. "They are Russian domovoi. We can talk about what I found out on the way back to the park. We'll take Oz's van."

The headache woke Willow. It pounded at her temples and covered her in cold, clammy sweat. She opened her eyes cautiously, hearing the skittering movement all around her.

She knew she was lying on the ground. She could tell that from the cold and irregular hardness pressing into her back. Slowly, she slitted her eyes and looked up. Bats hung upside down from the cavern roof far above her. As she watched, several of them opened their mouths and glared at her with greedy eyes.

Okay, this is so *not where I want to be.* She made herself remain calm, with effort. She trembled inside, but did nothing to attract the attention of her captors.

Glancing around, not moving her head but using her peripheral vision to its fullest, she spotted a dozen or so faeries flitting around the cavern. She wasn't able to figure out how big the cavern was, but she knew it was of huge proportions. Most of it looked natural, but tool marks scarred the walls as well. A child-sized doorway opened into another cavern to her left.

The faeries moved in the darkness, lighting candles in specially prepared hollows in the walls. A soft, golden incandescence filled the cavern. Murmuring faery voices created an undercurrent of noise that threaded through the area. The floral scents from the candles gave off a heady bouquet.

Buzzing sounded at the top of Willow's head. She closed her eyes tightly, trying not to breathe any differently than she had been.

"Foolish, Willow," an eerie voice intoned. *"We know when you're sleeping, and we know when you're awake."* Cold, cruel talons drew across her cheek. *"You must get up. We've been waiting for you to join us."*

"So this lantern has the whole Aladdin thing all over it," Xander said in the back of Oz's van. "Rub on the magic lantern, get a few wishes. Change your life."

Giles nodded. "Exactly. And there must be some truth to it. With that kind of power lying around, a number of people are going to be interested in acquiring it."

"Including the vampires," Angel spoke up quietly from the shadows. "They know about the power of the lantern too. That's why they're there."

"Yes," the Watcher said. "But the faeries are cold

and evil, and they have their own agenda for how things are going to turn out tonight."

And Willow's in the hands of those things, Buffy reflected, watching as Oz raced the van back to the side road where Willow had been taken from them. She gazed fearfully into the darkness.

The cold talons hooked under Willow's chin with amazing strength. She cried out in pain as the faery pulled her to her feet. Others flew over and dropped into formation around her.

"Follow," the faery commanded. He took the lead, flying only slightly ahead of her.

"Where's Oz?" she demanded, not moving.

"Don't try my patience, Willow," the creature threatened. *"You can walk or you can sleep. King Elanaloral wanted to meet you, to let you know of the great service you are going to do for us."* It glared at her. *"I didn't see that it was necessary, but he is our king."* He gestured.

One of the faeries behind Willow jabbed her in the leg with its spear.

Willow cried out in pain and grabbed her leg. The cut wasn't large, but it stung, letting her know the spear was probably coated with something. Reluctantly, she followed the faery's lead. The cavern was more illuminated now, filled with the soft glow and scents of the fragrant candles. She kept walking, and the sounds of her own footsteps sounded hollow around her.

* * *

"What are the faeries intending to do with Willow?" Buffy asked. "She showed up on their radar by trying to protest Gallivan Industries' involvement here. She's on their side."

"Yes. I'm sure that's what first drew their attention to her, but perhaps that's not what secures it now." Giles hesitated. "The faeries are adept at recognizing other beings with supernatural ties. They sought out the vampires long ago."

"Why not now?" Angel asked.

"Because they're not pure," the Watcher replied. "They carry the taint of evil with them. Plus, they're already dead."

"*Already* dead?" Oz asked. "You said, already dead."

"I think the faeries intend to sacrifice Willow," Giles told them, "to empower something the faeries call the Homestone."

Buffy wrapped her arms around herself, shuddering as a preternatural chill shook her.

Willow ducked through the small doorway in front of her, placing a hand against the cold, rough stone to keep her balance. The room beyond was an oval chamber that formed a rounded kind of arrowhead.

"*Enter, witch,*" a harsh voice commanded, "*that I might see you better.*"

Reluctantly, Willow walked into the chamber, guided by the spears of the guards around her. Her heart thumped in her chest, and goosebumps raised on the back of her neck.

At the other end of the room, blocked in by the two sides of the rounded arrowhead shape, a wizened faery sat on a carved wooden throne, tucked between the gaping jaws of a sculpted stone skull with hollow eyes. Glowing orange coals filled the empty eye sockets, lending the skull a baleful gaze that leaked down over the faery. He might have been two feet tall, if he'd been stretched out to full length, as tiny as any of his subjects.

"Come closer," the wizened faery ordered. *"I would look upon the wondrous being that Chammeus says will guarantee our return to the power due us."*

Wondrous being? That's a good thing, right? So why does this feel so not good? Moving closer was the last thing Willow wanted to do, but she felt compelled to do so. Her legs moved of their own volition. As she got closer, she got a better look at the old faery.

He looked like a sack of sticks, corpse-gray skin stitched loosely over the warped skeleton. A shelf of knobby bone stuck out over the close-set black eyes. His face was thin and blade sharp, though the large nose offset that impression. His fingers were bent and splayed, not fitting closely about the bone-and-jade scepter he held. A crown of twigs, twisted and fitted painstakingly together, sat crookedly on his narrow head.

"On your knees, child," he commanded in his brassy rasp. *"Know me as Elanaloral, king of We-of-Shadows. And obey me."*

Willow stood her ground on trembling legs. "Where are the children?"

Anger filled the old, haggard face, pinching it tight as the eyes slitted. *"You dare treat me so insolently?"*

"I want to know that the children are all right." Willow barely managed to keep a quaver out of her voice and maintain eye contact.

One of the other faeries moved forward nervously. He didn't, Willow noticed, try to make eye contact at all. *"Majesty, she does not recognize your power for what it is. She has been brought here only for her part in the rebirthing of the Homestone."*

"Take her," Elanaloral snarled. *"Bind her and make her ready for the agendum. The Homestone will again be ours."*

Willow tried to run, but there was nowhere to go. She was instantly surrounded by armed faeries.

CHAPTER 15

"**D**mitri's research turned up the first mention of the Homestone," Giles went on. "According to the translation of his document, and to one other I was sent, the Homestone was deeply important to King Elanaloral's own mythos. As you know from the cursory study we've done on the domovoi, they're hearth spirits, keepers and protectors of the home."

Buffy chafed under the delay, ready to get into action, where she did her best. Still, she knew enough to realize that she performed best when she had more information.

"The original domovoi Homestone held all the archives and records of the faeries," the Watcher said. "These compilations represent power, both imagined and real. Though never proven, legend suggests that a Homestone allows a faery family to make the most of the powers they wield. A focal point, if you will. In the beginning, the Homestone was created for each of a dozen kings, given freely by their creator."

"Who would that be?" Angel asked.

Giles shrugged. "No one knows. As you've heard, there are a number of legends that suggest the beginnings of the faery mythology. Pick one. Possibly it's as true as any other. At any rate, every resource I've found suggests that they are very hard to make."

"How?" Oz asked quietly.

"They're forged in the dark of the moon," Giles said, "and activated by using a witch's blood."

Witch's blood. Blood of a witch. Buffy exchanged a glance with Angel.

"Witches?" Xander exploded. "What do faeries know about witches?"

"Enough, apparently," Giles stated. "Some Russian legends borrow heavily from Hungarian folk stories. The tales of the Hungarian witch, Baba Yaga, come almost immediately to mind."

"Why witches?" Oz asked. Buffy saw the fear in his face and knew that part of him wanted to cling to the idea that Giles might be wrong.

"In Europe, perhaps druids were used," the Watcher replied. "But the requirements were the same. It had to be the blood of a human who was tied to nature the same way the faeries were, offering a little protection against iron weapons and because humans were more of the world as it is now than when faeries first appeared. I have no idea if this really works, but apparently the faeries believe it does."

"You're talking about human sacrifice." Oz's face blanched white.

"We've got civilizations in our history whose religious practices depended on human sacrifices," Giles pointed out.

"Then we've got no time to lose," Buffy said. She hauled weapons from the duffel bag. "I found everything I could that had iron. Like this staff." She twirled the six-foot staff effortlessly, causing the iron-capped ends to blur.

"Maybe you haven't checked," Cordelia said, "but the last time I looked, that forest area is huge. And it's probably crawling with vampires."

"I'm not going to sit this one out when Willow's life is at stake," Buffy stated. "No way that's going to happen."

"Maybe I've got something," Xander said. Quickly, he brought them up to date on his own activity regarding Baxter Security's office. He opened the notebook computer Cordelia had brought, then booted up the disk.

Buffy leaned in to scan the screen, taking in the map at once. "Why would Hutch be interested in this?" she asked.

"I don't know, but he was," Xander said. "He went there looking for it."

"Why didn't he look for it before?" Cordelia asked.

Xander shrugged. "Maybe he wasn't interested

until he found out about the kidnapped children. Maybe it didn't seem important."

"It's possible someone else has been searching for these faeries," Giles put in. "There are some local legends concerning them. From what you say about your friend Hutch's interests, it's possible he's put as much together as we have after hearing Willow's story."

"Meaning he's looking for Aladdin's lamp too," Oz said.

"Yes. As is, evidently, Hector Gallivan, according to Xander's tale." Giles clearly looked uncomfortable at the thought.

"Before or after he decided to build an amusement park here?" Angel inquired.

"An interesting conundrum, isn't it?" Giles asked, getting that faraway look in his eyes that Buffy recognized. The Watcher traced the map with his forefinger. "Assuming that these are maps charting the probable location of caverns beneath the forest, we may be able to assume that's where Willow has been taken."

"Which cavern?" Cordelia asked.

Giles traced the markings. "They all appear to connect."

"If it was that easy," Oz asked, "why didn't Gallivan find them?"

"I couldn't possibly answer that question," the Watcher replied. "Other than to tell you finding the entrance to those caverns is probably harder than it looks."

"Faery powers," Xander said. "Aren't they like the ultimate deceivers?"

"Some of them," Giles told him.

"Then let's go find out what's true and what's false," Buffy said, hoisting the staff.

Buffy peered down into the excavation pit she and Giles had escaped from days before, relieved when she saw no vampires at work inside. The others were spread out around it.

"I checked through the updates the archeological crew has been posting at the university," Giles said. "They didn't list the lantern as being found."

Buffy turned her head, scanning the surrounding treeline, her senses alert to the slightest movement or sound.

"It might not exist anymore," Xander pointed out. "If it was made of platinum, someone could have wandered off with it years ago."

"We have no choice but to believe it does still exist." Giles dropped into the excavation pit and snapped a military trenching tool together. "It's of faery origins. Even they would have a hard time destroying it. According to the reading I've done, it still holds power over Elanaloral and his clan. As long as it exists, they can be called back into the lantern by lighting the wick. And they can't destroy it without a Homestone to focus their powers through." He measured the ground with his gaze, then approached one of the walls. Drawing the trenching tool back, he sank the sharp edge into the earth at the side of the pit. "Perhaps if we find it, the lantern will provide us an advantage."

"We can't hang all our hopes on finding the lantern," Buffy said.

"Quite right." Giles continued digging, breaking up the clumps at his feet. He took a large flashlight from the pack he'd brought and switched it on. The ellipse of white light spilled out across the ground. He searched through the earth, turning up three arrowheads and the broken blade of a knife. "I downloaded the dig team's projected layout of the village and determined where the chief's tepee was. With any luck, we'll find the remnants of the lantern there."

"If they're to be found," Angel said, scanning the area from the edge of the pit. His tone of voice made it clear he believed that wasn't going to happen.

"Yes. So we'll temporarily divide our forces." Giles took up the tool again, slugged it deeply into the ground again. "Buffy, you and Angel and Oz will go on ahead to the area marked by Gallivan's terrain map. I will remain here with Xander and Cordelia long enough to pursue this objective for a time. The survey showed the excavation team was quite close to the chief's tepee when they quit."

"Not me," Xander said, shaking his head. "Willow's out there somewhere and I'm going after her."

Giles stared up at him. "Do you want to find her, or do you want to help her?" he challenged quietly.

"Why me?" Xander asked.

"Because I need help," Giles said. "If I'm to move all this ground and search it, I'll need another pair of strong hands. Cordelia can help search, but it won't be easy." He continued digging while he argued his case, piling dirt around his feet. "Buffy and Angel are best qualified to stage a rescue attempt inside those caverns. And I'm not prepared to ask Oz to stay behind. Are you?"

Xander glanced briefly at Oz, then shook his head. "No." He offered Oz his hand. "Bring her back, man."

Oz nodded and quietly said, "I will."

Xander dropped into the pit and joined the Watcher. "Let me shovel for a while, Indiana. You know more about what you're looking for."

"Do you know what mucking around in all that dirt is going to do to my nails?" Cordelia asked.

"Yes," Giles answered. "You'll find a pair of work gloves in my pack that should fit you. And there's a small metal detector as well. It has a loop of wire at the end of it. There's also a pair of walkie-talkies that we can use to stay in touch."

Reluctantly, Cordelia climbed down into the pit and opened Giles's pack.

"Watch your back," Buffy said. "Don't forget about the vamps."

"You be careful, too," the Watcher advised as Cordelia tossed Oz a walkie-talkie. "Faeries can be despicable creatures. We'll be along as soon as we're able."

Buffy turned and led Angel and Oz deeper into the forest. She carried the staff at her side, keeping it close to prevent it catching in the trees and brush.

* * *

Willow stumbled and fell, tripped by one of the faeries shambling along at her feet. She caught herself on her hands, barely preventing her head from slamming into the stone floor. Hanging on to her self-control by a thin thread, plagued by questions about what had happened to Oz and to Tad and the other children, she glanced around the new cavern she'd been guided to.

Elanaloral flitted between the stalactites. Huge burning candles made from beeswax and other natural substances threw garish shadows against the walls. The faery king perched on a ledge at the end of the huge cavern.

The sound of moving water gurgled up from the crevice in the center of the cavern. Willow guessed that it was from one of the underground springs in the area or a sea finger stabbing into the coastline from the Pacific Ocean.

Dozens of faeries lined the walls, nestling in carved hollows. They gazed at her in anticipation. A baby's plaintive cry echoed to Willow's left.

She stared into a small cave there and saw human children sleeping on a bed of dried grasses. All but one of them slept, a little girl about Tad's age. Then she rolled over and went back to sleep too. Willow pushed herself up, drawn by their helpless appearance.

Two faeries flew up and confronted her with spears. They hovered with beating wings.

"No," King Elanaloral said. *"Stay away from them."*

"I want to make sure they're all right," Willow said.

"They sleep," the faery king stated. *"Nothing more. We are not without compassion."*

"They're children," Willow argued. "They need to be with their families."

"They are here to aid us against the humans that would destroy this forest," Elanaloral said.

"Gallivan doesn't care about those children," Willow told him. "Don't you understand that?"

"These children belong to barons in Gallivan's court," the faery king said. *"This, we understand well. Humans have a tendency to care much about their children."*

"Their families do." Willow tried to think of a way to make the faery king understand. "Gallivan doesn't have any children. He won't care."

"Even so," Elanaloral stated, *"once the Homestone has been created, we no longer need to fear him. There is a power source here, the like of which we've never before seen."*

Willow gasped. *He's talking about the Hellmouth!* The existence of the Hellmouth was what kept the vampire numbers in the area at a high percentage. And it also drew some of the other craziness to Sunnydale.

"Now, after all these years, we understand why we were brought here. This power reached out for us, brought us to this place, and to you, who seem to have a tie to it."

Because of Buff? Willow wondered. After all, Buffy

179

blocked the creatures the Hellmouth attracted and loosed.

"Once we've tapped into this source, we will be undefeatable."

Willow didn't know if that was possible, but she was certain even trying wouldn't be good.

The faery king waved his scepter. *"See that she is prepared."*

Faeries surged forward to do his bidding, over-powering Willow easily.

Beating wings sounded overhead.

Buffy turned instantly, raising the staff so that one of the iron-capped ends pointed skyward. She watched an owl straighten out its wings and glide just above the treetops. Then it was gone.

"You okay?" Angel asked softly.

"Not quite to double-dip Rocky Road end-of-sale frenzy," Buffy admitted. "But close. Those things have *plans* for Willow."

"We'll get to her." Angel touched her shoulder reassuringly.

"I told Oz that," Buffy said quietly out of Oz's earshot. He walked behind them, staring intently at the map Giles had given them from the disk Xander had gotten. They'd printed it out in the van using Willow's laptop and portable printer. "That doesn't mean I believe it."

"Belief is something you choose to do," Angel replied.

"It's hard."

Angel gave her a gentle smile. "If it was easy, it wouldn't be worth as much."

"I think we're almost there," Oz called out. "We need to turn."

"Are you sure?" Buffy asked.

"Yes." He waved the map toward the stand of trees to the right.

Buffy looked to Angel, who peered into the darkness. "Any of our other friends around?"

The vampire listened and looked, then shook his head. "We're clear."

Buffy nodded at Oz, hefting the spear. With a werewolf and a vampire at her back, she would find Willow or hunt down the ones responsible. . . . *Don't even think that!* she scolded herself. "Lead the way, Oz. We'll follow."

Oz stepped up the pace, gliding through the trees. Buffy noted the predatory moves he made and wondered how many days to the next full moon.

In minutes, Oz guided them into an earthen cul-de-sac in the forest. It was a small ditch with four-foot-high walls topped by trees and brush. Grass clung to the walls, mixed in with the underbrush. No openings showed.

"Dead end," Angel said in disgust. He glanced around.

"No," Oz said. "This is it." He knelt in front of the right wall and placed a hand against the earth. "She's in here."

Angel took the map Oz had been looking at. After a brief perusal, he said, "Maybe." He drew his hand back and slammed it against the wall. A section of earth-covered wall fell back inside. Golden candle-light framed the narrow opening.

Oz shoved his head in and breathed deeply. "It's here."

"Let me in there, Oz," Buffy said. "And radio Giles. Tell him exactly where we are, what we've found."

"Sure." Oz stepped back. It was one of the things Buffy most appreciated about Oz. Where a lot of other guys would have gotten wrapped up in the whole macho thing of being the tough guy, Oz readily accepted her abilities.

Gripping the staff, Buffy hunkered down and climbed through the opening. Unexpectedly, she slid down, losing her balance for a moment.

Two faeries attacked her at once, winging toward her and slashing at her face with stone knives.

Xander thrust the shovel home again, only instead of the meaty *thunk* of noise he usually got, this time there was a definite *clank*. He banged the shovel experimentally, creating more clanks.

Giles pushed himself up from the latest load of dirt he and Cordelia had been sifting through. "Careful."

"Careful?" Xander asked sarcastically. "You're talking about a thing that's lasted maybe a couple hundred years, been across the ocean floor, and survived being buried. You think a shovel is going to do any damage?"

"It might," Giles replied.

Xander pulled the shovel away. "Oh."

The Watcher shoved small digging tools into the earth. "It feels big enough."

"Bigger than anything we've found before," Xander agreed. He was covered with perspiration from his exertions. In the last twenty minutes they'd turned up arrowheads, utensils, pie plates that were rusted through, and an assortment of galvanized cans that Giles told them had come from the 1930s or 1940s when local families had heavily camped the area.

Working delicately, digging around the object, Giles removed it from the earth. The ground was slightly damp and clumped together. The Watcher held the retrieved object in his arms and worked carefully. Slate-gray metal, untouched by rust, emerged, captured by the large flashlight Cordelia held.

A long moment later, Giles's expert hands removed the last of the clumped earth and revealed the lantern's ornate shape. It had been crafted in the shape of a bear standing on its hind legs. The light was supposed to stream from the bear's snarling mouth and eyes.

It wouldn't offer much light, Xander thought, *but maybe in Russia at the time it was the equivalent of a lava lamp.*

"Is that it?" Cordelia asked.

"Yes," Giles said. "I believe it is." He brushed more dirt away. "Ah, here's the inscription Dmitri wrote about."

"Really attractive," Cordelia said. "If you're into collecting tacky."

A shadow fell into the excavation pit, snaking down from above. Xander raised the trenching tool defensively. It was all metal, so it wouldn't serve as a stake for a vampire, but it might slow one down.

Only it wasn't a vampire.

"Hutch," Xander said so Giles would know. Cordy already knew him. Two other boys Xander recognized from the comics store flanked Hutch.

"Hey, Xander," Hutch said. "Mind if I take a look at the lantern?"

"Yeah," Xander said. "Actually, I do. We found it. I think we'll keep it."

Hutch lost his smile. "Can't let you do that, buddy. We need the lantern."

"Who's we?" Giles asked.

"We." Hutch pointed at himself and his friends. "A few others we brought along."

Xander stood on tiptoe and looked over the rim of the excavation pit. He saw shadows moving in the background, drawing closer. "Hutch isn't exactly what you think he is," Xander said over his shoulder. "It took me a while to figure it out. But I did tonight after he pulled his fade at the security office. Every time we went somewhere, this guy put away enough food for an army. And he's got a mean streak a mile wide. He embarrassed even me on occasion. And he's got these really weird, deformed forefingers. Everybody doing the math on that okay?"

"You believe he's a changeling?" Giles asked.

"Yeah. Probably in league with King Eggroll."

"No," Hutch said. "My group split away from Elanaloral a hundred years ago. Elanaloral wanted to stay with the old ways and remain in hiding, and he was afraid someone would find the lantern and succeed in calling us all back into it. We've chosen to live among you humans, replacing children who had promising futures and building our own power base. Elanaloral's kidnapping of the Gallivan children jeopardized that." His eyes flashed silvery in the darkness.

"How did it jeopardize you?"

"Elanaloral's activity drew attention to us," Hutch replied.

The changeling was lying and Xander knew it. "No," he said slowly. "That's not it. You didn't know where Elanaloral was, but you could have found out easily enough years ago. And it's not like he's going to give you guys up, or even know what you've been up to. Or like he'd even care. If you wanted to find him, you'd be there now. Not here. Wouldn't you?"

Hutch only stared at him with a stony gaze.

"It's the lantern, Giles," Xander told the Watcher. "They're here for the lantern. They're afraid of it."

"No more games," one of the other changelings snarled. He morphed, changing into a thin scarecrow with pinned-back ears and a mouthful of serrated teeth, and leaped down at Xander.

Holding the trenching tool in both hands, Xander swung at the changeling, hitting him full in the face and knocking him to the ground.

Roaring with rage, the changeling shoved itself to its feet. It came at Xander again.

Then it came apart, exploding in a flash of light

that seared the night. On the other side of where it had been standing, Cordelia raised the iron-tipped billy club Buffy had given her. "Iron, remember?"

"Yeah." Xander dove away as the other changeling hurled itself down, morphing during the plunge. It somersaulted in the air and landed on broad, clawed feet. By then Xander had his hands on the old iron sword he'd chosen from Buffy's arsenal. He yanked the weapon from the leather sheath and sliced through the changeling.

Immediately, black infectious lines threaded through the faery. It fell to earth, and landed bonelessly. A moment later, all that was left was a shiny black ooze that quickly soaked into the ground.

"Fools!" Hutch yelled. "Now you're gonna die!"

Xander set himself and gripped the sword in both hands. "Bring it on!"

Other changelings raced from the trees.

"Maybe," Giles suggested as he picked up the iron-headed club he had, "you were a bit overzealous in your challenge."

Before the line of changelings reached the excavation pit, more shadows crowded from the surrounding countryside. It only took one glance at the bestial morphed faces and fangs to let Xander know what they were. The vampires intercepted the changelings.

Absolute carnage reigned as vampires and changelings battled to the death and undeath. Apparently the vampires couldn't bite the faeries, but it didn't stop them from rending the creatures limb from limb.

From the roared curses, Xander gathered this was a turf war, or maybe some of the vampires had banded together in their own pursuit of the legend of the faeries.

Whatever it was, he decided to take advantage of it. He pushed Giles and Cordelia into motion. "C'mon. Spectators probably get handed out as hors d'oeuvres." They scrambled over the far side of the excavation pit and ran in the direction Buffy and the others had gone, hoping the faeries' and vampires' pursuit would be slowed just long enough for them to get there.

CHAPTER 16

Buffy ducked beneath the stone knives the faeries thrust at her face. She swept the staff up, automatically adjusting for the narrow confines of the tunnel she'd stepped into. She rammed the iron-capped end at one of the faeries and watched it slam against the wall. Before the dazed creature's dropped knife could fall to the ground, she brought the staff around in a short arc again and hammered the second faery.

She stepped back from them and watched as black lines spread through their bodies. Black ichor was absorbed into the ground where the two faeries had once been.

"Now that's biodegradable," Buffy said.

Angel dropped down after her, glancing only for an instant where the faeries had been. "There are going to be a lot more where those came from," he advised. He wore a small iron buckler on his left wrist only a little bigger than a personal pan pizza. He carried an iron cudgel in his other hand.

Oz followed them, putting the walkie-talkie away. "Giles said they found the lantern, and they're on their way here, but there's another problem." He quickly explained the situation with the vampires and the changelings while Buffy led the way deeper into the tunnels.

The faeries pinned Willow against the ground. On his perch above them, Elanaloral raised his hand and gestured. Slowly, tree roots pushed up through the rocky earth and coiled around her wrists and ankles like rough-skinned snakes.

"Don't," Willow pleaded, feeling the rough bark curl against her skin. "Don't do this!"

"We've only just begun," the faery king told her. *"There is still much you must give us. The Home-stone must be made anew."*

Willow glanced at the sleeping children in the cave. She tried desperately to think of anything that would free her. She yanked against the root coils but succeeded only in abrading her wrists. The roots exuded a syrupy sap that stung her.

Elanaloral dropped from his perch, clutching something in one hand. He flapped his gossamer wings, hovering in place only a few inches above her. Opening his hand, he showed her the object. *"The Homestone,"* he announced. *"At least, it soon will be. And this one, after I bind it to the power that resides below us, will be more powerful than any made before it."*

Willow gazed at the stone in fascination. Tiny glyphs marked its exterior in a hundred different patterns. All of them were hypnotic in their intensity. Some glittered with glassy silicon bits while others held various colors. Each line that twisted and whorled around the stone seemed to have a story to tell; and each intersection seemed to build on the stories that went before it.

"I've spent these last hundred years in my study of this phenomenon," the faery king said. *"If it weren't for the earth-wreckers plaguing us now, I wouldn't be so hasty in attempting to bend those elemental forces to my will."*

"You're talking about the Hellmouth," Willow said. "It's very powerful, and very bad. If you do something wrong, you may destroy your whole group here." *And more,* she thought. Tampering with the Hellmouth could be like a nuclear disaster. Only there was no telling how far effects could spread or how long they'd last.

"The presence of the earth-wreckers gives me no choice about waiting," Elanaloral stated. *"The Homestone must be made so that we might destroy the lantern before it is used against us."*

"What about the children?"

Elanaloral gazed at her with a bemused expression. *"You worry about the safety of the children over your own fate?"*

"I just want to know they're going to be okay," Willow said.

"They'll be cared for," the faery king said. *"Raised as our own and taught to revere our ways. We can*

train them to serve the same purposes as changelings, and spy on the humans that could hurt us."

"That's not what should happen to them," Willow argued. "That's not right."

"Right," Elanaloral said, *"is in the hands of the strongest. What I say as king of We-of-Shadows is right, and this is what I decree. Even the foul and barbaric tongue of you humans allows me to be that clear."* He took a stone dagger from his belt. It was tri-bladed, coming together like a Y.

Willow knew from her studies of sacrifices made in religious orders that the blade was designed to pierce the offering and bleed it to death in short order by keeping the wound open.

Elanaloral raised the dagger. *"Good-bye, witch. Take pride in knowing your offering will allow us to live unfettered ever again."*

An arrow flew at Buffy's face while two others went wide of the mark. Even as she ducked away from it, Angel threw his arm out in front of her protectively. The arrow sank into his arm up to the leaf fletchings.

Buffy scooped three iron shot from the leather bag at her waist. Each one was about half the size of a Ping-Pong ball. Still in motion, the Slayer stepped back into the tunnel around Angel. Her arm whipped back then forward three times quickly.

Two of the iron shot hit the three faeries and turned them to black ooze puddles. The remaining one turned and fled back down the tunnel, screaming out an alarm as the iron shot whizzed by it.

Buffy glanced at Angel as he pulled the arrow from his arm. "Are you okay?" she asked.

He nodded. "Yeah, but I thought he had you." The arrow slid out of his flesh, leaving behind a bloodless wound that would be healed by morning.

"Thanks."

"No problem." Angel flexed his arm, making sure it still worked well enough.

Buffy took the lead again, holding her staff in both hands. The way was well lighted by candles, and that had surprised her at first. Then the arrangement sunk into her mind, making her realize they were placed for ritual effect.

Oz kept them on track by using the map Xander had gotten. The tunnel suddenly forked ahead of them and Buffy slowed.

"Which way?" she asked.

"Just a minute." Oz consulted the map, turning so he got the best light coming over his shoulder. The walkie-talkie buzzed for his attention. He reached for it automatically. "Yeah?"

"We're at the opening," Giles said, breathing raggedly, "but I'm afraid we're only yards ahead of our pursuers. Have you found Willow?"

"Not yet. Just follow the main tunnel to catch up with us." Oz ran a finger along the map.

A burst of movement from the tunnel to the right was the only warning Buffy got. She turned, whirling toward Oz, grabbing his shirt with one hand and yanking him to the side of the tunnel. She folded the staff under her arm, shortening its length and making it easier to use in the tight confines of the tunnel.

Angel blocked one of the attacking faeries with the iron buckler, slapping it to one side. The creature blackened and puddled against the wall. He batted another out of the air with the cudgel, and caught another one with a backhanded blow. Four of them whipped by him.

Buffy jabbed one of the faeries in the face, feeling the brunt of the impact shiver along her arm. Then she whacked another one with a swift slashing stroke. Unfurling the staff, she slammed into the third one, knocked it aside.

The fourth one shrieked and dove for her face, carrying a spear in its two tiny hands.

Working on reflexes, the Slayer roundhouse kicked the faery, knocking it to the floor. Windmilling the staff around, Buffy brought the iron cap crashing down on the dazed faery. It puddled.

"Path of most resistance," Buffy said, racing down the tunnel on the right.

"This is it," Oz said a moment later. "I can hear her."

A huge, intense buzzing sound echoed down the tunnel. The noise reminded Buffy of a special on bee-keeping she'd seen with Willow when they had channel-surfed one quiet night.

A half-dozen other faeries tried to intercept her, but she was moving too fast for them to stop her. She was among them before they knew it, and the iron-capped staff slashed without mercy. Three of them fell to her skill, and Angel and Oz dealt with the rest.

"No!"

Now Buffy heard Willow's voice ahead. She

pushed herself harder, throwing herself into a power slide through the low door ahead of her. She skidded across the ground on her side, her left hand out wide of her body.

The next cavern was huge, filled with candles and faeries. Buffy spotted the really ancient-looking one with the knife above Willow. She also saw the coiling roots wrapped around Willow's wrists and ankles.

The old faery, Buffy assumed, was Elanaloral, king of the faeries. He turned his attention back to Willow, raising the knife again and starting his strike.

Still on her side, Buffy drew the staff back and hurled it like a spear. She didn't aim for the old faery, uncertain if the staff would get there in time to knock him away from Willow before the blade buried in her heart. She threw for the blade itself.

Sparks flared when the iron-capped end connected with the knife. The blade sailed from the withered and tiny hand, followed immediately by the faery king's outraged shout. He leaped into the air, winging after the tumbling blade. The staff smacked into a faery on the other side of the room and reduced it to a black puddle.

"Kill her!" the faery king ordered.

Buffy didn't know if he was referring to her or Willow, but neither was acceptable. She somersaulted to her feet and dropped into a defensive half-crouch. More than a dozen faeries winged at her, waving spears and knives and tiny swords.

She gave herself over to her reflexes. A heel thrust sent one of her attackers flying, an elbow smash countered another as she spun, sending it flying into a third. She leaped to avoid arrows shot at her feet, and turned that into a series of kicks that sent four more of them tumbling head over heels. It didn't kill them, but it blunted the attack and gave her a few precious seconds of respite.

Then Angel was in the room beside her. His speed caused the faeries to split their attack. His iron-bound cudgel battered them to black goop as he fought his way to her side. "Buffy!" He shook the ironclad buckler from his left wrist and threw it to her.

Buffy caught the small disk in both hands.

"Vampire!" one of the faeries shrieked. *"They've linked up with the humans! Put a stake through his heart and kill him!"* A trio of faeries put arrows to bowstrings.

Estimating the distance and the angles in an eyeblink, Buffy threw the buckler like a Frisbee. It caromed from two walls, then shattered two of the faery bows. Rebounding from another wall, it collided with the third faery archer, killing it.

Buffy flipped again, dodging over a pair of faeries streaking for her legs with keen-edged stone knives. She came down on her hands, managing to grab the staff in her right hand. When she came up to her feet, she placed her hands on the staff little more than shoulder length apart.

She went into an offensive kata, moving on sheer speed and reflex, not thinking about anything except survival. She couldn't stop every faery attack and received a half-dozen cuts from bladed weapons that would require treatment but weren't life-threatening. The staff moved in her hands like a live thing.

Angel fought like a dervish, ripping through the faeries grouped against him, never staying in one place long enough for them to succeed against him. He used all the floor that was open to him.

Oz scrambled through the doorway and raced to Willow's side. He pried at the root coils holding her prisoner, breaking chunks of them off. Willow pulled against the roots, trying to free herself.

Buffy stayed in motion, swatting at the faeries, noticing there weren't as many of them as there had been. The survivors started to cluster against the cavern's roof, putting distance between them.

In the next moment, Giles, Xander, and Cordelia joined them. Giles wielded his club with a fencer's deft skill, making definite, telling strikes rather than batting full-tilt the way Cordelia and Xander did. He also carried a bear-shaped lantern in one hand, and Buffy guessed that he'd successfully recovered the prize he was after as well.

Once Xander was at Willow's side, he sawed at the roots with his sword blade, cutting them easily. He and Oz gathered Willow and pulled her to her feet.

"This way," Cordelia cried, defending the small doorway through which they'd entered the cavern. Without warning, a creature Buffy didn't recognize reached through the doorway and seized Cordelia's ankle. Cordy yelped in surprise but maintained enough presence of mind to whack the offending arm. It turned to a black puddle just like the other faeries, despite its bigger-than-faery size.

Buffy slapped another faery from the air, puddling it. "What was that?" she asked Xander.

"Changelings," Xander replied, not breaking his concentration from the battle. "Think of them like new and improved Klingons from *Next Generation*. *TV Guide* synopsis: think of them as bigger bad guys. They've been insinuating themselves into our world for a hundred and fifty years. That one may have been my new ex-buddy Hutch."

More of the changelings and vampires followed the first, flooding into the room, taking away the available space. The good thing was they occupied the regular faeries' attention as well.

"There's another way out," Oz called.

"Where?" Buffy asked, grabbing her staff again. Even with her Slayer metabolism and increased strength and speed, she was starting to wear down. The faeries could win because of sheer numbers alone.

"According to the map, there's a tunnel on the other side of this wall," Oz said, pointing to the wall behind Buffy. "The wall's not supposed to be very thick."

Twisting, the Slayer peered at the wall, noticing the stress marks and the gaps in the stone. Concentrating, she spun and kicked at the wall. Cracks fissured the stone and rock dust puffed out over her.

"Stop them!" the faery king ordered. *"They mustn't be allowed to escape!"*

The faeries redoubled their efforts to swarm Buffy.

"I've got your back," Xander said to Buffy, lifting his sword and pulling Cordy over to them at the same time. He slashed at a faery, slicing into it and turning it to glop.

Buffy drew back her leg and kicked again. The wall crumbled, tumbling down in chunks and a haze of rock dust. "Open sez-a-me." She turned and grabbed Willow, looking at Oz. "Where does this tunnel go?"

"Up. It must be some kind of abandoned shaft or a natural cavern." Oz took a big flashlight from his belt. The corridor beyond the hole in the wall held only darkness; there were none of the candles the faeries had put up. He took Willow's hand and started through.

"No," Willow said weakly. "The children. We've got to save the children."

For the first time, Buffy spotted the small alcove against the far wall and realized what it held. "We'll get them."

More vampires and changelings fought their way into the room, creating a lot of confusion and driving the faeries back. Buffy led the way across the room. Oz took one of the six children, cuddling it easily and confidently in his arms. He had the flashlight clipped to his hip. Willow took another one, followed by Xander, Giles, Cordy, and Buffy. Backing out of the alcove, they headed for the tunnel.

"Ugh," Cordelia complained. "Does somebody want to trade me one that isn't wet?"

"Move," Giles urged.

Angel operated on the perimeter, using his cudgel on faeries and changelings to destroy them and beating the occasional vampire back into the thick of the battle.

They went through the opening in the wall as quickly as they dared, holding the kidnapped children close. Giles, Cordy, and Xander added their flashlight beams to Oz's, illuminating the twisting, rock-strewn path ahead of them.

Angel covered their backs, an effort made much easier by the narrowness of the corridor.

As she ran, Buffy was totally conscious of the small baby she carried. She wondered briefly if it was Maggie's son, but she didn't unwrap the blanket to find out. The baby belonged to someone who missed it very much and that was all she needed to know. She cradled it against her, protecting it from the rough stone around them with her body.

Less than a minute later, she smelled the cool night air again, no longer just the foulness trapped in the caves. She glanced ahead and saw Oz batter his way through a tangle of roots and dense brush. The others followed, going through more easily now that Oz had cleared the way.

But if it hadn't been for Angel, the faeries would have overtaken them. Buffy knew all of that was about to change once they emerged into the open. Then the faeries' movements wouldn't be restricted.

"Giles," she called as she raced out of the tunnel. When the Watcher turned around to face her, she handed him the child she carried. "I'm going to need both hands free. Keep the others moving." She pulled the staff out in front of her, wondering how they were going to get to the cars so far away while carrying the kidnapped children.

Angel tried to hold the faeries trapped in the tunnel, buying them extra time. But he was battered back, pierced by a dozen tiny arrows that came close to his heart.

Buffy whirled the staff, finding targets immediately. As she felt the thumps against her weapon, she tried to figure out exactly where they were in relation to the rest of the park.

"The backhoes," Giles said. "They're not far away. They can provide some protection."

"What about the security guards?" Xander asked.

"With all the vampire activity in the woods around us," the Watcher replied, "I really doubt there's much chance of them bothering us." He took the lead, moving up to a jog even with the babies in his arms.

The children slept on despite the activity around them, and Buffy guessed they were still under the faeries' spells. *Lucky kids.* She kept her staff in motion, defending against attacks and sweeping away any faery that got within whacking distance. Her arms grew tired from slinging the staff around. Perspiration covered her body and soaked her clothes as fatigue started to become a real factor in their continued survival. A glance at Angel told her he was in the same shape.

She used more of the iron shot she carried to knock down any faeries that managed to get past her and Angel. Her aim was mostly true, but there were occasions when the shot missed and broke branches overhead.

They reached the collection of equipment in less than two minutes. Following Giles's direction, they huddled under one of the road graders, tucked away almost safely between the giant rubber tires. Oz, Willow, and Cordy cared for the babies, keeping them covered on the ground where they'd had to lay them. They still hadn't woken.

Buffy, Angel, Xander, and Giles battled any faeries that tried to get too close. Beyond the perimeter of their own battle, the one involving the vampires and changelings escalated. Evidently some of the vampires had picked up on the fact that fangs and claws weren't as potentially damaging to the faeries and changelings as the Slayer's and Slayerettes' weapons were and had found pieces of iron around the excavation pit. For their part, the changelings and faeries pierced the vampires' flesh with arrows, getting better at targeting their hearts on the fly.

"Staying here is definitely not an option if we're going multiple choice," Buffy told Giles.

The Watcher nodded, his own face streaked with blood, sweat, and dirt. "The lantern," he said. "The lantern has to be lit." He took it from his belt and passed it across. "They'll be drawn into it."

Buffy whacked another faery between the eyes, turning it into a rush of glop that plopped against the big tire beside her. Other faeries banged against the road grader's sides. "You're sure?"

"The lantern reportedly still has powers over these

creatures," Giles said. He looked at her, breathing raggedly, then shrugged. "It's really my best guess at this point."

Buffy whomped a vampire in the head when it tried to reach in for her. Although she hadn't killed it, the vampire staggered back and was attacked by a changeling that shoved a length of broken branch through its heart. As the vampire turned to dust and the changeling turned its attention to her, she said, "Okay, we go with the best guess." She grabbed the wire handle of the lantern Giles offered. "Got a match?"

A look of surprise filled Giles's face. He patted his pocket and shook his head ruefully. "No," he admitted.

Xander snaked an arm back and flicked a Zippo open. The lighter's flame jetted up at once. "Come on, baby, light my fire."

Buffy snatched the lighter, then took a deep breath. Up on the balls of her feet, she dashed out from under the road grader and ran into the clearing. Faeries attacked at once, but she batted them away with the staff. When a vampire threw itself at her, she vaulted over its back and kept going.

Then Angel was behind her, standing guard defiantly, his shadow painted over her as she placed the lantern on the ground and dropped to her knees. He battled everything that came at her, holding nothing back. Only a few feet away, she spotted the bodies of two security guards. *Gallivan's people definitely aren't going to be a problem.*

She found the catches on the bear-shaped lantern

and opened the small door. Dark soot stained the lantern's interior, caked on from decades of neglect. But there was nothing inside to light. No wick, no fuel.

Glancing quickly around, aware that she and Angel had become the eye of the storm raging through the forest, Buffy reached up and ripped a section of a vampire's shirt away before Angel staked it through the heart with a branch he'd picked up. The vampire turned to dust as she poked the material inside the lantern. She flicked the Zippo and the cloth caught slowly, burning only around the edges at first, but not fully igniting.

"No!"

Buffy looked up and spotted the faery king winging her way. He held a spear in his hands, aiming directly at her. She immediately felt better about using the lantern. *You know you're doing the right thing when the bad guys get mad.*

Although she wasn't able to bring the staff around and make contact with the ironclad end, she blocked the faery king's attack with the wooden haft. The creature caromed off, but got control of himself again. He reached into the pouch at his side and pulled out a fistful of glittering dust.

Buffy knew she'd have to abandon her position if the creature flung the sleep dust. She took out her last two iron shot and hurled them as quickly as she could. Another faery dove in front of Elanaloral, sacrificing itself for the king.

Buffy turned her attention back to the lantern. She breathed gently on the embers clinging to the material, willing it to catch fire. A moment later, flames twisted up from it, throwing off gray smoke and crackling.

"No! This cannot be!" the faery king howled in outrage.

In the next breath, it seemed like a tiny nuclear explosion went off in the lantern. Flames filled it, and light jetted out through the bear's eyes and mouth, forming cones of light in the darkness. Waves of heat washed over Buffy, blowing her hair back and making her squint.

And the faeries came at once, drawn like moths to a flame. They flew into the light by the dozens, shrinking down to microscopic glowing specks and diving into the lantern. Even the changelings were affected by the lantern. Several of them recognized the danger and tried to get away, but the mystical energy caught up in the lantern reached out for them, dragging them into the maelstrom of lights as well.

The vampires drew back, obviously afraid they were going to suffer the same fate.

Then, as suddenly as the lights had started, they ended. The bear's eyes and mouth turned dark, and the fire in its belly died away. Unwilling to leave the lantern there, Buffy reached for it hesitantly but found it was cool to the touch.

She grasped the wire handle firmly and stood, holding it up for all the vampires to see. "Scavenger hunt's over," she told them in a harsh voice. "I'm not letting go of the lantern and it's standing room only in there already." The last was said bravely, ignoring the exhaustion that threatened to sweep her away.

The dozen or so vampires she could see among the trees grumbled and looked at one another, searching for a leader. But no one opted for the job. Quietly, they filed away, melting back into the shadows.

Buffy hated letting them go, wishing she was able to slay them all now, but there was no way.

"You okay?" Angel asked, touching her arm.

"Yeah," Buffy replied, glancing at the road grader as Giles led the others cautiously out from under the machine. "We put the faeries away and we got the kids back, so I'm going to chalk this one up as a win."

"It was," Angel said. He put an arm across her shoulders and helped support her.

Despite the hurt and fatigue that filled her, Buffy's spirits rose immediately when Giles handed her one of the babies.

"They're awake," the Watcher said gently. "They woke just as the light in the lantern dimmed."

A smile touched Buffy's lips as she looked down at the small round face almost covered by the blanket. Wide, tiny brown eyes stared back at her innocently as the little boy gnawed at his fist. He wrapped his other fist around one of her fingers, squeezing tightly.

"C'mon," she told the others, "let's see about getting these little guys home. It's way past their bedtime."

EPILOGUE

"So Hutch never showed up at the comics store?" Buffy asked. She sat on one of the stone picnic tables flanking the play area in Weatherly Park. It was Friday evening, and the unsanctioned Sunnydale High Spring Blow-Out was in full, frenetic swing.

"Nope." Xander sat on the bench near her. Both of them watched Cordelia circling through the crowd, awarding style points and demerits to the little group of wannabes that trailed after her.

"Did you ask about him?" Buffy asked. She was still tired from the previous night, but was making the occasional circle through the woods around the party to make sure no vampire party crashers gathered. So far she hadn't tripped across a one.

"Casual like, you know," Xander answered. "They said Hutch's friend had called in and told them his father was on his deathbed in Scranton or someplace and Hutch had to go. Hutch never mentioned a father to me."

"So we don't know if he's in the lantern or got killed during the turf war." Buffy had given Giles the lantern for safekeeping.

"No. But I don't think we got all the changelings. I think some of them are still among us."

"Now there's a creepy thought."

"Must be the company I keep," Xander replied in mock seriousness. "How are the babies doing?"

"I called Maggie," Buffy answered, "and she said Cory's doing just fine. She's talked with some of the other moms who had missing babies, and they're all doing great. No health problems." Last night after leaving the park, they'd taken the babies to the hospital, left them outside the emergency room entrance, and called from across the street. No one had taken a relaxed breath until the orderlies took the babies inside.

The media still hadn't gotten ahold of that story. But they were playing up the "wild animal" attack that had killed seven Baxter Security guards in the employ of Gallivan Industries. A lot of parents hadn't liked the idea of their kids showing up for the Blow-Out in the park where the attacks occurred, but that just made interest in the party even bigger. The turnout was mondo huge, and Cordelia was enjoying her queen bee status.

The thing that had captured most of the media attention was Hector Gallivan's decision not to go ahead with his plans for the amusement park. That attention increased even more when Gallivan refused to comment further.

Willow's sympathizers in the adult and business worlds who had been interested in her campaigning told her that Gallivan was pulling out because of the security guard murders. The first couple he'd been able to write off as accidents.

Now the tabloids were starting to hang around Sunnydale and generating stories that grew more and more outrageous. A handful of television magazines had even showed up to interview some of the people at the Blow-Out. Buffy watched them circle through the partying groups and knew that the stories would be even wilder by morning.

And none would be even close to the truth.

Oz and Willow joined them, carrying extra cups of punch and balancing two plates crammed with snacks. "You guys are missing a great party," Willow said. Now that baby Tad was back where he belonged, her mood had brightened considerably.

"Not me," Xander said, gazing at Cordelia. "I'll get to hear about it again and again later. Blow by blow. Who wore what, who was hanging with who, and why some people just don't belong on an invitation list."

"Yummy," Willow said. "I know you can't wait."

Xander flashed her a sour look. "I just wish events like this with Cordelia didn't seem like so much work."

"She looks like she's enjoying herself," Oz said.

"Oh she is," Xander replied. "It just kind of

leaves me hanging. At least I've got company. Buffy's sitting out as a wallflower too."

Buffy put her chin on her fists and her elbows on her knees. What Xander said was too true. She'd been looking forward to the party, but now it didn't live up to her expectations.

"You don't have to be a wallflower," a low voice said in a tone that sent a shiver up Buffy's back.

She turned around and saw Angel standing there, dressed in black and looking as hot as ever. "Hi."

"Hi." He looked a little uncomfortable now. "I probably shouldn't have come. In fact, I was planning on not coming. But I kind of ended up here anyway."

"I'm glad you did," Buffy said. But it hurt her to see him, knowing things could never be the way they had been between them. *Still, can't they be that way for a couple hours?* She looked at him. "You said something about me not being a wallflower."

Understanding, he offered his hand. "Would you like to dance?"

"More than anything else I can think of at the moment," Buffy replied, and she let him lead her out into the cleared space under the strung lights where other couples danced. She took him into her arms when he reached for her, and they swayed together.

And for a short time, the Slayer knew peace. There was no past and no future, only the comfortable now.

ABOUT THE AUTHOR

Mel Odom lives in Moore, Oklahoma, where there are *reportedly* no vampires. But there's lots of interest in finding out everything there is to know about them. And some people around the neighborhood do mulch their gardens at the oddest of times.

In addition to writing for *Buffy,* he's written books in the fantasy, SF, computer gaming, comics, action-adventure, and horror fields, including titles for *Sabrina, the Teenage Witch, Allen Strange, Young Hercules,* and *Alex Mack,* as well as the novelization of *Blade.*

His e-mail address is denimbyte@aol.com, and he enjoys corresponding with readers.